Wasn't it bad enough his brother had been wrongly convicted? Now they were trying to hang a rap on him...

"You and your brother are very clever. He's been convicted of murder himself—"

"Oh, so, in your esteemed opinion, the inclination to murder is something that's in the genes?" Linc took a step in Emilia's direction. "First of all, my brother was wrongfully convicted—*wrongfully*—and secondly, that's one of the most inane things I think I've ever heard in my life." Linc took another step toward her.

Emilia resisted the urge to back up, as she didn't want Eisenger to know he'd gotten to her and that she was a bit frightened by the anger in his voice. She threw a grateful glance at Howard as he took hold of Lincoln's upper arm.

"Hang on, man. No need to threaten the lady," Howard said.

"She's no lady and I didn't threaten her." Lincoln spread his arms and grinned but to Emilia it appeared to be more of a grimace than an actual smile. "I'm an innocent man standing in his own driveway being needled by an officer of the law. Maybe I need to make a call of my own to the police commissioner. Tell him all about the harassment I'm enduring based on the mere fact that I have a brother in Angola and I have a dead law partner who I couldn't possibly have had a chance to kill. What do you think?" Linc glared at Emilia. "How do you think that phone call could affect that gold shield that I bet you have had for about five minutes?"

"You don't have that kind of clout, mister. If you did, your brother wouldn't be in prison now, would he?"

At that comment, Lincoln did lunge at Emilia. She whipped her gun up and aimed it directly at his chest.

She thought she was ready for the hard cases, but that was before she met him…

Emilia Hammond recently earned her gold shield as a detective with the New Orleans police department and is working on her first assignment, eager to prove herself capable of handling her promotion. After a series of attacks on prostitutes in the French Quarter, she finds herself going undercover to investigate. In the process, she's called to the scene of a murder at an attorney's office. She has a good lead, a solid case, until her prime suspect turns the tables on her.

He's trying to clear his innocent brother, and now he's a murder suspect himself…

Attorney Lincoln Eisenger is from a prominent New Orleans Garden District family. His brother Myles is in Angola Prison for a murder he didn't commit. Linc is determined to clear his brother's name and bring him home. But when his law partner is killed, Linc becomes the prime suspect. Now he has to clear himself as well as his brother, all the while trying to ignore the sparks igniting between him and the spunky female detective he thought was a prostitute.

KUDOS for *The Eisenger Element*

In *The Eisenger Element* by Sherry Fowler Chancellor, Emilia Hammond has just earned her detective's badge. Now she has to prove that she's worthy of the promotion and it wasn't just because she has several family member on the force. So when she gets called to the scene of a homicide, and everything points to Lincoln Eisenger as the prime suspect, Em pounces on him as the murderer and is blind to everything else. However, she can't ignore the sparks flying between them. Linc, on the other hand, is trying to prove that his brother was wrongly convicted of murder, and he doesn't appreciate some smart aleck new detective trying to blame him for killing his law partner when he wasn't even there. While he is more than a little attracted to her, her prickly personality and bad attitude prove they have nothing in common—but lust, even if they are both too professional to act on it. Add to that the fact that Em has been working undercover as a prostitute, trying to solve the murder of one, and you have a very complicated situation. Chancellor's characters are well-developed, realistic, and charming. You just can't help rooting for Em, even when her gung-ho attitude gets her in hot water. The plot is strong and the story fast-paced. And the sweet little romance between Linc and Em give this cozy mystery a little extra punch. ~ *Taylor Jones, Reviewer*

The Eisenger Element by Sherry Fowler Chancellor is a cute, clever cozy mystery combined with a sweet, wholesome romance. Our heroine, Emilia Hammond, has been newly promoted from patrolling a beat to homicide detective. Since her grandfather, father, and brothers are all with the New Orleans Police Department, too, Emilia is determined to prove herself as the youngest homicide detective in the history of the department. Investigating the murder of a prostitute, Emilia goes undercover, walking the streets, looking for a motive for the murder of one prostitute and the brutal beating of another. Our hero, attorney Lincoln Eisenger, has a soft, compassionate heart and wants to help prostitutes get off the streets and find another way to make a living. So when he sees Emilia dressed and acting like a prostitute, he thinks she is underage and tries to help get her off the streets. Which, of course, is the last thing she wants. And when she is called to a homicide scene at Lincoln's office, she finds evidence pointing to him. But her over-zealous attitude and firm belief in his guilt without any evidence that he can see gets his back up. Since his older brother was railroaded for a murder he didn't commit, Lincoln is convinced that the New Orleans PD has set him up to take the blame for the murder of his law partner. The fact that these two are very attracted to each other only complicates an already complicated case. *The Eisenger Element* is well-written with strong characters, lots of fast-paced action, and some very unexpected villains. I love it when I can't figure out 'who done it' until the author reveals it. Like my collection of Agatha Christie novels, this is one you'll want to keep and read again and again. ~ *Regan Murphy, Reviewer*

ACKNOWLEDGEMENTS

I want to give my thanks to the city of New Orleans. It's always been an inspiration to me. From the people, to the architecture, to the food, it's a veritable gold mine for a writer's imagination. The city is like no other in the United States and is a character in itself.

The Eisenger Element

Sherry Fowler Chancellor

A Black Opal Books Publication

GENRE: COZY MYSTERY/ROMANTIC SUSPENSE

This is a work of fiction. Names, places, characters and incidents are either the product of the author's imagination or are used fictitiously, and any resemblance to any actual persons, living or dead, businesses, organizations, events or locales is entirely coincidental. All trademarks, service marks, registered trademarks, and registered service marks are the property of their respective owners and are used herein for identification purposes only. The publisher does not have any control over or assume any responsibility for author or third-party websites or their contents.

DEDICATION

This one is for the men and women who work to keep New Orleans safe for those of us who love to visit: the NOPD.

Chapter 1

Leaning nonchalantly on the lamppost outside the law office where he worked, Lincoln Eisenger pretended to smoke the cigarette in his left hand. He glanced down at his steel Rolex where it rested on his right wrist. It was almost time for the girl to walk past, if she kept to her normal schedule. He wasn't sure exactly what he planned to do to try to rescue her, since he wasn't really equipped to go up against an unknown pimp, but something had to be done. The urchin had to be under age fifteen and she sure didn't need to be on the streets selling herself.

Why he was compelled to try to rescue this particular child was a mystery to him. He'd lived in the Garden District of New Orleans his whole life and, when he left his safe neighborhood, he saw so much decadence and crime, as well as prostitution, he'd thought he was immune to it. Linc couldn't fathom why this one small hooker preyed on his mind but she did and he made a point each work day to be on the street when she passed. One day he was going to get the nerve to question her and find out which pimp was putting minors on the streets. What he'd do with that information was unclear.

He'd once had a grand plan to fix some of the ills of this place but that had fallen apart when, first, his father died, and then, shortly thereafter, his brother was arrested for murder.

Linc knew a few cops he might call to aid this young girl but most of them didn't like him, since he sometimes had to ask them hard questions on the witness stand. He knew they might not relish working with him when so many times they were on the opposite sides in the court-room.

"What are you doing? You've been out here every day this week." Linc's law partner, Clifford Van Nuys came by and stopped beside the lamppost. "I didn't even know you smoked. How have you kept that a secret? We've been partners for a while and I had no idea."

Linc held up the cigarette. "I'm faking it."

Clifford threw his head back and laughed. "As a sen-ior partner and one of the founding members' great-great-great-grandsons, don't you have the right to take a fifteen minute break without pretending to have that vile habit?"

"I can take a break whenever I want. It's really not your business what I'm doing, is it?"

"Whoa." Clifford held his hands up in front of his

face. "Where'd that come from? I'm merely shooting the breeze and you take off my head?"

"Sorry. I'm a little tense. I've got to head out to Angola later and I always get a bit anxious when it's time for that." Lincoln tried to keep his temper but it was difficult. Clifford hadn't been particularly supportive when Myles had been convicted and sent to Angola prison for a twenty-five-to-life sentence.

"Man, I sure am sorry about your brother. I know it's gotta be breaking your mamma's heart to see him out there."

"Mom never visits him. She pretty much disowned him, as you well know." Linc flicked the ashes from the cigarette. If this buffoon didn't go away soon, he'd still be here when the child prostitute came by and all hope of talking to her to offer assistance would be gone. He really disliked Van Nuys and hated that the man was a partner in the firm founded in 1840 by the Eisenger family. Linc had voted against making Clifford a partner but he was the sole dissenter of the other nine partners in the firm. Even Myles cast his vote to allow the man to be a partner before going to prison. Linc wasn't sure why the man rubbed him the wrong way but the mere sound of his voice made him cringe inwardly.

"Sorry about that but I guess she has her reasons." Clifford smirked. "Like a son committing murder. Not something a grand dame of the Garden District wants in the family tree, is it?"

Linc barely controlled the urge to punch the man in the face. Yes, Myles had been convicted of murder but he was innocent and it was Linc's mission in life to prove that fact and to get him released. "Keep your mouth shut about my family, Van Nuys."

"Or what?" Clifford's smile was smarmy and Linc wanted to erase it from the jerk's face. "What do you think you're going to do about it?"

"Hey, guys, what's going on?" Tamela Jones, another lawyer with the firm, strolled up with a plastic bag in her hand. "You both look like you want to kill each other."

"I think Linc wants me dead, for sure." Clifford took hold of Tamela's free arm. "Escort me inside to my desk? I feel safe with you."

Linc held back his breakfast that threatened to expel itself on the sidewalk as he watched the bald man try to flirt with the sexy red-haired newest associate. *Please.* Did the man think he actually had a chance with the young lawyer? She had brains and looks and could have any man she wanted. She sure wouldn't settle for the paunchy jerk of the firm.

Tamala looked back at Linc. "I'm going to take Cliff in and eat my take-out at my desk. You can relax your fists now." She disengaged herself from Van Nuys and turned to open the door. "See you later. I wanted to run some figures by you before I send a settlement letter on the Myers case."

"Fine. I'll be back from Angola later this afternoon." Linc glanced down. Yep, he had fisted his hands. He hated to think that he might have actually struck the man right here in the street. He decided to make a better effort to get a grip on his emotions before he did something he would, most likely, regret.

As soon as they disappeared into the building, Linc faced west down the sidewalk since that was the direction he'd seen the child come from the last few days. He hoped he hadn't missed her while his jackass law partner had him distracted.

In a few moments, the girl he wanted to save strolled into view. It broke his heart to see someone of her age dressed the way she was. She had on fishnet stockings that had a long tear along one thigh, a pair of over the knee black fake leather boots, and the shortest pair of shiny purple shorts Linc had ever seen. The young hooker also wore a short, cut-off white T-shirt that exposed her belly and an outrageous red wig with a riot of curls flowing down her back. It was clearly a wig, as God never intended any real human being to have hair that color.

The over the top make-up she sported only served to emphasize that she was underage. Way too much purple eye shadow and false eyelashes didn't add one year of age to the child. Lincoln was disgusted to think about the men who paid to have encounters with the young girl. She didn't even have breasts yet, for God's sake.

Linc watched her progress down the sidewalk as she

slung her hips in what she must've thought was a provoc-
ative way, but was really kind of sad. When she was almost upon him, he tossed the cigarette to the ground and
stubbed it out with the toe of his Italian loafers.

The girl stopped in her tracks and, tapping the toe of
her high-heeled boot, glared at him. "This right here is
what's wrong with this city."

Stunned that she spoke to him with such anger in her
voice, Linc took a step back. "What?"

"People littering the streets with their cigarette butts,
spilled drinks, and even vomit. I swear this place gets
worse every year."

Her words struck him as hilarious. What was she?
Fourteen? And she thought the city was worse every
year? What would she think when she was the ripe old
age of twenty?

"What the hell are you snickering about, mister?" she
asked.

"Nothing."

"It had to be something or you wouldn't be doing it."
The girl stepped right up to him and with her chest almost
touching his stomach, she snarled, "Back off and leave
me be."

"I wasn't doing anything. I was out here taking my
break and minding my own business."

Dear God, how had she gotten him on the defensive
like this? Wasn't he supposed to be soothing her and telling her he wanted to help her out of her predicament?

How did she turn the tables around so fast?

"You were messing up my city with your litter." She backed up and pointed at the sidewalk. "Pick it up and throw it away in a proper receptacle."

"What kind of prostitute cares about litter?" Lincoln couldn't believe the question came out of his mouth. He didn't mean for it to fly out like that but it was curious that this girl would care so much for the state of the sidewalk.

She gaped at him for a moment, as if lost for words, then shook her head. The red curls swayed in the slight breeze from the river. Recovering from whatever silenced her, she snapped, "This kind of prostitute." She leaned closer. "Did you want to have a good time?"

"No. I want to help you. I can assist you in getting out of that life. I want to get you and others like you off the streets." Linc held his hand out as if to take hold of hers. "Will you let me help you?"

"What are you, some kind of do-gooder? Why would you want to help me? I don't even know you."

"You're underage. I'm sure you probably ran away from home and didn't know this was how you'd end up. I'd like to get you and any of your friends in the same situation off the streets. I can offer you some help."

She recoiled from him, turned, and broke into a run. He watched as she turned the corner, amazed that she could run so well in those high-heeled boots. As she disappeared from view, he realized he'd probably blown any chance he had of helping her. She probably wouldn't come back this way ever again.

As he moved to enter the building where he worked, he knelt down and picked up the cigarette butt. Remembering the oddness of a prostitute caring about litter, he scratched his head with the hand that held the butt, leaving the scent of tobacco on his hair.

∽∾∽∾

"Shoot, shoot, shoot, shoot, shoot." Emilia Hammond strode up the stairs of Precinct Five in the French Quarter. She stomped her feet so hard, her boots sounded as if they were puncturing holes in the risers. Once on the second floor, she turned the corner, pushed open the swinging half-gate leading to the bull-pen, and snatching the red curly wig off her head, flung it on her partner's desk.

"Bad day, sweetie?" Howard Mills shoved the wig away from his cup of tea that he was stirring some sugar into.

"You bet. There's some crusader out there who thinks I'm an underage hooker and he wants to get me and my little friends off the streets." Emilia said the last words in a sing-song voice.

"I bet that went over well with you. Did you kick him in the nuts?"

"No. I ran away."

"*What?* The great Emilia Hammond ran from a do-gooder? My illusions of you as a ball-buster are crushed."

She flopped down in the green metal chair next to Howard's desk with her legs sprawled across the space between it and the next desk. "I would've stayed behind to crush his soul but I'd already screwed up and almost gave away my undercover operation."

"How's that?" Howard took a sip of his tea.

"The stupid clown had thrown down a cigarette butt."

Howard put his hand over his mouth, but Emilia could see some of his tea spurt out between his fingers. "Don't laugh at me," she warned.

"I can't help it. I ain't never seen nobody like you when it comes to cigarettes." Howard had swallowed his tea. "Why do you get so up in arms over them things?"

"You know they killed my grandma. She could never kick them. Granddaddy gave them up but she couldn't get free. I wish they were against the law. The least I can do is try to make people see it's not a good thing to smoke."

"So, this do-gooder who wants to rescue you is a smoker?"

"Yeah. I've noticed him outside that one office building around the corner. He seems to be out there every time I go past. The bad thing now is that I need to avoid that area but I also need to be around there in order to investigate this case we have." Emilia snapped her fingers. "Wait. I know what we can do."

She grinned over at her partner.

"Oh, no, honey. This skinny dark-skinned man is *not* going to go in drag to stroll the boulevards just because you messed up with your pretty little self."

"I can't help it if I look like I'm twelve." She glanced down at her chest. "You think these will ever grow in?"

"It would be weird if they did since you're a little mite of a thing, so be glad you're not out of proportion like poor old Barbie."

"Funny. I don't want to be a mutant like her but it would be nice to have cleavage."

Howard smiled. "Only on Saturday nights. The rest of the week you'd want to be built exactly like you are so you can take down some bad guys without anything getting in the way."

"You're right, and speaking of those bad guys, what are going to do about *Mr. I Want to Save Underage Hookers*? He's going to get in the way of this investigation. I know that as well as I know that I'm sitting in an uncomfortable green chair that's as old as me."

"Want me to talk to him?"

"What are you going to do, dress as my pimp and put a whipping on him?" Emilia grinned. She scratched her scalp vigorously. That wig really hurt.

"My mamma would say whupping, not whipping."

"Either way. Is that the plan?"

"I don't think so. We really can't take a chance on

him interfering with the case. I think we have to avoid that area of the city." Howard held his hands up. "Hang on. I know what you're going to say and yes, I know, you have to stroll that street as well as the ones around it. What I'm suggesting is that when you're ready to head that way, that you radio me and I'll take a walk down there and distract your man. We can't give up and I think that'll work." Howard half-rose from his seat. "Let's go talk to the captain about what's up. He may have a better suggestion on how to deal with your would-be rescuer."

"Sit down. Let's not bug the captain. We can handle *Mr. Expensive Clothes* ourselves."

"If you keep changing his name, I won't know who we're trying to outsmart, Emilia."

"I'll make a playbook like my brothers' football coach did in high school. How would that be?"

Howard grinned. "That would be a good thing. Just so I don't get confused."

Emilia leaned forward with her elbows on her thighs and looked her partner in the eyes. "Don't be an idiot. Everyone in this precinct knows you could give Sherlock Holmes lessons in sleuthing. You put on that *oh shucks* persona but anyone who spends more than ten minutes with you knows you're the one to beat on smarts. You have every player in place and can read most people in five seconds flat."

"I've been fooled before by some pretty smart criminals but I think I can figure out your rescuer quickly. I need to amble down the street and see what's what. Go wash that gunk off your face and change into your street clothes. We'll go for a po-boy and you can show me which building he works in. Maybe we can get a glimpse at him from afar."

"Sounds good. I'm famished." Emilia stood. "It'll take me a few minutes. Be right back." She clomped back down the hallway to the locker room where she grabbed her jeans, white blouse, and blazer to change into after her shower.

Once she was clean and dressed, Emilia tucked her service weapon in the back of her waistband, drawing on her jacket to cover it. She ran her fingers through her wet hair, grateful that she'd inherited the texture of her mother's blonde hair and a little bit of the curl from her father's kinky hair so she could wash it and go. No muss, no fuss. She slipped on her black rubber-soled work shoes and tied the laces. Leaving the locker room, she returned to the bullpen to the sounds of the other detectives whistling and cat-calling at her.

She took a bow and shouted, "You like Emilia the homicide cop better than Amy the Hooker?"

"Hell, no, but that Amy girl would charge us for each whistle," one of the guys in the corner yelled.

"You got that right and well she should. She's a working girl," Howard called out as he took Emilia by the elbow.

"Let's get out of here. I'm famished and these guys

are obnoxious." Emilia made sure she said the words loud enough for the rest of the squad to hear.

They headed down the stairs to the exit. Emilia led the way toward the street. She sure didn't want the well-dressed man who'd stopped her on the sidewalk to prevent her and Howard from solving their latest case. She hoped Howard's plan would work to get the guy out of her hair so she could roam freely on her quest for her murder suspect. Proving herself as a capable homicide detective was imperative. As the youngest member of the team, it was vital that she succeed.

Chapter 2

The po-boy restaurant they chose was on the corner where Emilia turned to run to the precinct after her encounter with the man they sought. She really didn't want to see him again but she wanted to be able to show Howard where to go and which lamp post the guy made a habit of leaning on every day. The only way her partner could help was if he could identify the man.

They entered the restaurant, Joe-Don's, and approached the counter to place their orders. Emilia ordered a roast beef smothered in gravy and Howard ordered a shrimp po-boy. They each got a cup of chicory coffee and took a seat at one of the wobbly, beat up wooden tables with red-checkered grease cloth tablecloths on them. It wasn't a fancy place but they made a wicked good sandwich.

When their food came, Emilia cut her po-boy in half

and grabbed the roll of paper towels. She pulled about ten off and stacked them beside her plate.

Howard nodded at her sandwich. "You always get the messiest one."

"That's why they made napkins, my friend." She picked up a handful and waggled them at him. "Best sandwich ever." She tucked one of the napkins into the top of her shirt.

"A bib? Why do you always embarrass me with that?"

"It's a white shirt and I can't be responsible for how you feel." Emilia picked up her sandwich, ready to take a big bite but before she could, she noticed movement at the door to the restaurant. She put her food down. "Crap, crap, crapola."

"What?" Howard moved his head.

"Don't look. Don't look."

"What is it?"

"Not what. Who. It's the guy." She ducked her head down.

"What guy?"

"The one I was going to show you where he works. He's at the counter ordering. What if he sees me?"

"So what if he sees you? He'd never recognize you now. You don't have on the red wig, you're dressed conservatively, and you're about six inches shorter without those heels. Eat your lunch and act naturally. You're not even on his radar." Howard grinned. "I, however, find I need to use the men's room. If you recall, it's right past the counter. I'll get a chance to look at him and then when I see him when you're undercover, I'll recognize him." He stood and leaned the knuckles of his right hand against the tabletop. "Can you sit here alone and eat like a normal person while I check him out?"

"Of course I can. I *am* an adult, you know."

"Sometimes I wonder." With that, Howard strolled over past the counter and down the hallway to the men's room.

Emilia worked on eating her sandwich and bent her head, watching the man through her eyelashes. He waited at the counter and, in the moment, Howard passed him on his way out of the men's room, the guy took his order in a to-go bag and left.

Howard returned to the table. He whistled under his breath.

"What?"

"We know that guy, Em."

"We *do*? How?"

"He's that guy who has the brother—"

"Whoa. That narrows it down. Yeah. Sure. A brother."

"Very funny. Let me finish my sentence, please."

"Whatever. Go on." Emilia took a huge bite of her roast beef. Gravy plopped down onto her plate.

"He's one of the Eisenger brothers. You know? The city's most eligible bachelors." Howard made quote marks in the air as he said the words. "Until one of them was arrested and convicted of murder that is."

"Oh, God. I didn't even recognize him."

"I wouldn't expect you to. You were still on the beat when all that came down. I recognized him immediately because I was a witness once in a case where he was suing for damages for an injury to his client in a bar fight. He's a tough nut and he really raked me over the fire— not even coals—it was a true trial by fire. I tell you, I'll never forget that man."

"Interesting that he would be concerned about a hooker, isn't it?"

"Maybe he wants to atone for his brother's sins?"

"I don't know about that. It's a bit odd if you ask me. It seems like I heard somewhere that he's trying to prove that his brother was wrongfully convicted. I don't think that would leave much time for prostitute saving. It's very curious. I wonder if he's some kind of closet pervert."

"Lord, girl, you're suspicious of everybody." Howard picked up his own sandwich and took the first bite.

"It's what I do."

Howard nodded as he chewed.

"While you finish eating, let's go over what we know already." Emilia pulled her police-issue notebook from her jacket pocket and flipped to her case notes. "We know the victim worked the few blocks around here as a hooker and she was underage. We have a general idea that she had some regular customers who also worked on the same block. We have zero idea who her pimp is— what with the three girls we've questioned all giving different answers." Howard poked the end of his sandwich at Emilia. "If I was a betting man, I'd put my money on Little Jim. He's the one with the most young gals in his stable."

"Okay. I'll jot him down as the next person we have a conversation with. You almost ready to go jack him up?" Emilia made a note in her book and then went back to reading her notes. "We also know she was killed sometime during the hours of nine and ten a.m." She looked across at Howard. "Call me naïve, but I thought most hookers were ladies of the night. What's this daytime hook-up about?"

"Yeah, you're naïve like I'm a white man. Neither of those is true. You aren't thinking about it the right way."

"What's the right way then, smarty?"

"A man who has a wife and kids, or one who has to be home at night for some reason, would want to get his jollies in the daytime when the misses thought he was busy at work. Busy working his dick would be more like it." Howard placed his napkin on his plate after wiping his mouth. "I think we're looking for a reputable businessman who can't be out trolling the streets in the evenings."

"All right, then. Maybe we need to start questioning some of the businessmen who work in this area." Emilia winked. "Maybe we can start with Eisenger. Could be he wants to rescue young prostitutes because he has a guilty conscience for killing one."

"I see two problems with that." Howard stood and, grabbing Emilia's plate as well, headed to the trashcan to toss in their napkins and stack the dirty plates in the bin.

She came up behind him, putting her notepad back in her pocket. "What's that?"

"One is that you didn't even want him to glimpse your face in here so I can't see how you plan to question him and the other is that I can't imagine a man who is fighting so diligently to get his brother out of prison would do something as stupid as killing someone himself. The last thing he'd want is to be moved into Angola as his sibling's roommate, right?" Howard opened the door and they walked out into the afternoon sunshine.

"Those are two very valid points but, as we both know, people can be incredibly idiotic. I say we head over and have a word with the man."

"Are you going to wear a bag over your head?"

"No. Like you said, I look entirely different in these clothes than my alter ego, Amy. No need for a sack disguise."

"I don't know, Em. This guy's pretty astute. He may recognize your pretty face with its splash of freckles across the nose. Perhaps you should stay downstairs while I go up and chat with the man."

"Pfft. You give the man too much credit. Come on."
Emilia stalked down the street toward Lincoln's office.

❧❧❧

Pulling in to the parking lot at Angola prison, Lincoln Eisenger took a deep breath. God, how he hated to
be here. Life had definitely handed his brother a bad set
of cards. How he'd ever been convicted of the murder of
a local man who worked at the parish clerk of the court's
office was beyond comprehension to Linc.

When Myles was arrested, Linc had been shocked
but there was never, in his mind, any chance that there
would be a conviction. When the jury came back with the
verdict, Linc had almost had a seizure. He recalled now
in the car exactly how it had gone down. He really
thought he'd stopped breathing and the blood ceased running though his veins in that moment. It got even worse
when the courtroom deputies pulled Myles out of his seat
beside his defense attorney and took him out the back
door to a holding cell.

Realizing he was about to hyperventilate, Lincoln
shook off the memory and opened the car door. Being the
only person who came to see his brother was tragic as
well. He still couldn't get over his mother disowning her
son. What happened to unconditional love? Linc snorted.
There was no such thing in the mansions of the Garden
District.

Grabbing his briefcase, as well as the empty bag from Joe-Don's to toss in the garbage—so his car wouldn't smell like Tabasco and onions from the sandwich he'd eaten on the drive up—he steeled himself as he stepped out of the automobile. Time to put on his encouraging face. It was getting harder and harder to give Myles hope that he would someday soon walk out of this place a free man. Linc and George McMann, the investigator he'd hired, were doing their best to find out who really killed the courthouse clerk but it was looking less and less promising that they would be successful in that endeavor. All roads were leading nowhere.

Thankful that he had a Louisiana bar card and could visit anytime he wanted as his brother's attorney of record, Linc bypassed the long line of visitors in the lobby waiting to be screened. He approached the guard near the lawyer's entrance and passed him his driver's license and bar card.

The officer inspected the identifications as well as the items in Linc's briefcase and then let him pass into the first set of gates. When that gate clanged shut behind him, Linc jumped a little. He was used to the procedure, but that clang always made him shudder a bit. He reminded himself that at least he could get out at the end of his visit.

When the first gate was completely shut, the second one inched open as Linc waited in the little vestibule formed by the two closed gates. When it was fully open,

he stepped through and greeted his escort. "Good afternoon. I'm here to see Myles Eisenger."

"Yeah. We got him. They radioed ahead for us to
bring him down on a walk and talk. He's already in interview room one."

The term walk and talk always made Linc smile a little. That was lingo for the inmates to be brought from
their cells to talk to their lawyers. He didn't know what
they called it when the families came to visit on regular
visiting days since no one in his family ever came.

The officer escorting Linc unlocked the interview
room and opened the door. "You know to pick up that
phone when you're ready, right? Someone will come get
you to lead you out then."

"Thanks. Yeah, I know the drill." Lincoln took a
deep breath and exhaled it slowly before he walked in the
room. He said a little prayer, asking for the strength to
face his brother as the changed man he had become since
being locked up and losing hope for the future. He took a
step inside and glanced over at his little brother on the
other side of the table dressed in the khaki-colored prison
shirt and baggy pants. It wrenched at Linc's gut every
time.

"Any news, Linc?" Myles asked. His face was pale
and, if possible, the bleakness of his expression was even
more heartbreaking then the last time Lincoln had seen
him, which was only a week prior.

What to say? How could he bear to tell Myles there

was really no change this week? There was nothing he could do but to say the words. Linc pulled out the chair across from Myles. "Sorry, man. No news." At the look on his brother's face, Linc added, "We're trying really hard to find another witness. It's slow going but we're not giving up. No way. I'm going to keep fighting until we're successful in getting you out and back to work."

"I find that I don't much care anymore. I've got to accept that I'm here for the duration. You need to let it go, bro. You can't waste two lives over this mess."

"What the hell are you talking about? Waste two lives?"

"Mine and yours. Mine is already over but you have a chance to live. You need to forget about me and find a woman to settle down with and give you babies. We need to salvage the family name and the only way to do it is to make a new generation to carry on the family legacy. I'm the black sheep and, if you let me serve my time without rocking the insular world of the Garden District, I'll be forgotten and the Eisengers can rise to the top again."

"Nonsense. You're talking nonsense." Linc opened his briefcase and pulled out a file. He knew these interview rooms were under surveillance and, even though the prison officers weren't allowed to listen to what was said due to attorney client privilege, they monitored the activity taking place inside. He knew he needed to appear to be talking about Myles's case or the powers that be might decide to disallow one-on-one personal visits if they thought he was merely coming to see the inmate as a family member.

"I'm not. It's not nonsense. It's what's good for the family."

Myles pulled at his left earlobe. It was a gesture Lincoln recognized. Light dawned.

"Ahh, I see." Linc nodded and pointed to something in the file he'd opened. Myles looked at where Linc pointed. He knew the game as well as Linc. Pretend to work the case.

Myles sent a sidelong glance at his brother. "You see what?"

"Caroline Eisenger Phelps, who said she'd never visit her murderous son has been here plying her black magic hasn't she?"

"I've never understood why you hate her so much. She's right, you know. I'm a black mark on the family. I need to be forgotten."

With great effort, and only because he knew he'd be booted off prison property if he laid a hand on an inmate, Linc resisted the urge to shake some sense into his brother.

Myles had always thought their mother was perfect and she did give the appearance of perfection. Slim, blonde, and always fully manicured and primped out, she exuded the old money of New Orleans, but the truth was, she married into the wealthy Eisenger family and transformed herself from the lower middle-class girl from Metairie, Louisiana, who spoke gutter English, to the upper class, cut vowels of the Garden District.

His mother was a charlatan, posing as a fine lady. Linc had learned that at an early age when he heard her speaking to someone at the side door of the mansion his family owned on First Street. She was crude to the person and her voice had an edge and accent to it that Linc hadn't heard before, and so it stuck with him. When he asked her about it, she tried to brush off the encounter but his memory of that moment stayed in the back of his mind from that moment on. She always said that her parents had died before she went to college and the boys had never met their maternal grandparents.

"Please tell me that you don't really believe that crap that she spews. She's only concerned about her husband's political career. I'm still convinced she was involved with that Phelps scoundrel before dad even died. She sure did marry him in haste. For someone who's always been so interested in having the perfect family, she needed to look at how that appeared to the greater New Orleans metro area. Dad wasn't even in the family crypt four months before the wedding."

"You know she said it was because Phelps was running for senate and it would be better for him to have a wife on the campaign trail than a girlfriend sitting at home."

"Yeah, right. Phelps needed a woman who looks good in a blue suit standing on a dais next to him when the adoring crowds waved after his speeches. Don't be fooled by all that. Mother wanted the attention. Make no mistake about that." Lincoln patted the file on the table. "Forget what she says. You're the only immediate family I still have. I refuse to give up on you and you need to keep the faith."

"I have no faith left, bro. I find that it's easier to exist in this place if I accept the lot handed to me."

"That breaks my heart, Myles. I want you to want to get out of here."

Myles snapped his fingers. "Oh, guess what? I almost forgot to tell you."

"What? Sounds like something good by the little touch of excitement I hear in your voice."

"I think you probably know that the inmates here do a rodeo in October, don't you?"

"I've heard of it but have never come to see it. What about it?"

"I'm going to ride in it on Sunday."

Lincoln couldn't believe it. He gaped at his brother for a few seconds. When he found his voice, he said, "You're going to *what*?"

"Ride in the rodeo." Myles actually smiled a real smile. Probably the first one that Linc had seen on him since the day he was convicted. "You know I *do* know how to ride a horse. I did dressage as a kid and a teenager. Competed even."

"Well, of course, you did but that is not the same

thing as riding in a rodeo. That's crazy. Your riding style is sedate and stylized. Rodeoing is an entirely different thing."

"It's a sport on an equine. What could be so different? Besides, we've been practicing." Myles raised his eyebrows. "You wanted me to have hope, didn't you? Can you try to understand my thought process here? If I'm going to spend twenty-five to life here, I need a hobby. Something to keep me busy. I mean, I could be a lawyer for some of these people in here who've asked me to help with their appeals but I find that I no longer love the law like I once did—I mean since it betrayed me and let me end up here."

Lincoln hadn't heard his brother speak with such passion in a very long time. If this rodeo thing was what it took for his brother to find some peace with the unfair life he'd been handed, then Linc would get behind it. "Will you be roping calves?"

"Maybe next year. This year since I'm new, I'm going to be acting as a rodeo clown. I've been practicing some barrel racing but it's too soon."

"I hope to have you out way before next October." Linc packed the file back in his briefcase. He knew his time was almost up in the interview room.

"I hope so, man but if you don't, I will at least have something to keep my interest. It seems that those of us who participate in the rodeo get to work in the stables all year. Even though I've never been a fan of mucking out stalls, since it gets me outside some, I can deal with it."

"Don't be fooled, bro." Lincoln stood and picked up the phone and called for a guard to escort him out of the prison. "You've been busy mucking out stalls in the practice of law for a long time. We seem to shovel a bunch of horse droppings around all the time in the courtroom."

The door opened to a corrections officer ready to accompany Lincoln. As he turned to leave his brother alone in the hated place, Linc held his breath. This was always the worst part. To his surprise, Myles was laughing.

"You got that right, Linc. We've shoveled a lot of crap in our time." Myles's laughter followed Lincoln all the way down the corridor.

Chapter 3

Emilia and her partner arrived at the building that housed the law firm of Eisenger, Eisenger, and Boutwell at the exact moment that a red-haired woman in a green dress and impossibly high heels came barreling out the front door.

She almost careened into Emilia who threw her hands out in front of herself to stop the woman's forward momentum.

"I say, ma'am, what's the rush?" Howard asked.

The lady's mouth moved but no sounds came out. Wild-eyed and seemingly disoriented, she gathered her balance on the teetering heels and reeled down the street, almost as if she were drunk, which was no surprise on the streets of New Orleans.

Emilia shrugged and stepped over to the threshold leading to the lobby of the building. "Come on. She's just another statistic in the Irish pub population. She most likely drank her lunch and wandered into the wrong building. Let's go."

Inside, they flashed their badges at the security man behind the counter. "We need to see Lincoln Eisenger," Howard said.

"I'm not sure he's in. He came in earlier today but there is a back door that the employees can use. He sometimes goes in and out that way." The guard spun the sign-in book around to face them. He held up a pen. "All visitors must leave their names."

Emilia signed for herself as well as Howard. "Did that woman who ran out of here sign in?" Emilia perused the list for names ahead of hers. She didn't see another woman's name for the whole day. That was odd. Unless the lady was a friend of the guard or something. Maybe she was visiting him and didn't need to sign in.

"I didn't see anyone." The guard's ears turned red which Emilia knew could be a sign of lying but what was she going to do to the man? She didn't care if he entertained ladies on the sly.

"Some chick, jumped up on something or plain ole crazy, darted out that door right there in the last two seconds and almost ran my partner down. Are you saying you didn't see her, son?" Howard asked.

The guard pulled himself up to his full height. "First of all, old man, I ain't your son and, secondly, if I say there wasn't anyone here, there weren't no one here."

"I'm going to find out who she was and why you're

lying to me but, right now, I'm heading up that elevator and going to have me a chat with Mr. Eisenger."

Howard spoke to the guard in the tone of voice that Emilia knew was trouble. Her partner didn't get angry often but, when he did, it was an interesting thing to see. Howard would be getting this man in a whole world of trouble before the day was done.

She knew he hated insolence and this rent a cop had it oozing out of him.

As soon as they were in the elevator, she pushed the button for the fourth floor when she noticed on the board hanging beside it that the firm was located there. To try to jolly her partner out of his bad mood, she said, "Old man, huh? I told you that you needed to color that premature gray out of your hair."

Howard ran his hand over his short-cut afro that was about one-third gray. "Man. I hate to think you're right. I'd like to keep it. I'm only thirty-five but the ladies seem to like a little salt and pepper on my noggin."

Emilia laughed. "I guess it's a good thing you want to attract the ladies then and not burly security guards."

"I'll let you know if I change my mind about what I like in my bed. If I wanted to, I think I could convince candy-pants down there that I'm the best lookin' man he's ever seen."

"I know you could but let me say, for the record, that I hope you'll stay with your main girl, Marsha. She's good for you."

He winked. "And I'm good for her. The best she's ever had."

Before Emilia could answer, the elevator door opened to a scene of chaos and carnage. Emilia and Howard both pulled their weapons and held them down to their sides. Each stepped off the elevator carefully and on high alert.

There was a pudgy man lying in a pool of blood and a woman in a gray suit kneeling over him. She had blood on her skirt and the pantyhose that covered her legs. Her shoes had dragged some blood around the area. It seemed to be drying on them.

Another woman in a suit stood over them talking on a phone and Emilia could tell by what she was saying that she was on the phone to the 911 dispatcher. Emilia pulled out her badge and held it up. "NOPD. Is the building clear?"

As Howard fanned out past Emilia with his gun drawn to protect the crowd from any perpetrator still in the area, the lady on the phone said, "Wow. You got someone here fast. There're two plain-clothes cops here already."

The woman turned to replace the phone on the cradle. Emilia called out, "Wait. Let me have that."

Howard continued his sweep of the room. Emilia could hear him asking the others who were in the main room where everyone else was and if there were any others in the building who didn't belong. She took the receiver with her free hand. "Dispatch? This is Detective Hammond. We're on the scene here but we're going to need backup, crime scene techs, and an ambulance." The victim looked dead to her but she wanted to ask for the ambulance as opposed to the coroner's van in case there was a chance to save the man.

Emilia replaced the receiver and turned to the woman who had been on the phone. "What happened here?"

"I don't know. I work back there." The woman pointed down the corridor. I heard Maggie scream— that's her over there leaning over Mr. Van Nuys—he's one of the partners here and she's the receptionist. Anyway, I heard her scream and I guess everyone else did too since we all seem to have run in here at the same time. I was the first one to grab the phone to call you. How *did* you get here so fast anyway?" The lady's voice quavered but she seemed to be holding herself together well.

"Did anyone see what happened? Do you think the person who did this is still here?" Emilia turned to Howard who had returned to her side. "Anything?"

"No. Everyone here appears to belong at the firm and I see no one with blood on them except the lady over there by the victim." He turned as the elevator door opened again. Two paramedics pulling a gurney stepped off. They were followed by a couple of uniformed policemen.

"I think her name is Maggie. At least according to this lady—" Emilia turned to the woman she'd been speaking to. "—I'm sorry, what is your name?"

"I'm Greta Greensboro. I'm the legal assistant for Lincoln Eisenger and you're correct, that's Maggie Stewart over there. Like I said, she's the receptionist. Mr. Van Nuys must have come off the elevator and collapsed. I don't believe anyone here would do that to him." She glanced around the room and Emilia followed the same path with her eyes. The area wasn't very large but was quite plush and it was obvious that the firm enjoyed great wealth. The tan carpet was a thick pile and the burgundy leather furniture was expensive and offset by the hunter green walls and pictures of fox hunting scenes. There were two hallways leading off the main reception area and Emilia decided that they needed to search them as quickly as possible in case they hid a killer.

"We'll have to question everyone," Howard said. "Is there a conference room we can gather them in so they won't contaminate the scene? And maybe an extra office where we can conduct our interviews? We'll also need to search the rest of the premises." He turned to the two additional uniformed officers who'd joined them. "You guys go handle that."

"Sure," Greta said. "We can put everyone in the conference room. I can offer you the snack room for interviews. My boss isn't here at the moment but I can't offer his office since there are confidential client files in there. The best I can do is to let you use the little kitchen we have that has a few tables for firm members to eat lunch or dinner as the case may be. It's this way." She turned toward the hallway.

"Hang on a sec." Emilia held her hand up and called out to the room in general. "Attention everyone. Please head to the conference room. Don't touch anything. We're going to have to print you all, as well as question you, since we need to narrow down if there are any strange prints here and we need to see if anyone saw anything unusual. Thank you for your cooperation."

One the men in suits, whom Emilia presumed was a lawyer for the firm, said, "You may not need our prints since this is a lobby area and I bet there are a lot of unknown prints here. We have clients in and out of this room all the time. Seems like a waste of resources to me."

"Since you appear to know so much, *sir*, you can be our first interviewee." Emilia didn't even try to keep the sarcasm out of her voice as she turned to the older of the crime scene techs. "Lou, how long you been doing this job?"

"About twenty-five years. Why?"

"Do you think we should skip that whole fingerprinting thing because there are a bunch of unknown people who may pass through this lobby—people who have to check in downstairs with the security guard on duty who clearly is more interested in signing people in and out rather than—I don't know—actually providing security? Do you think lawyer-man here in his gilded cage has any idea, and I mean *any* idea, what your job and mine entails? Like how the most tedious of tasks may somehow—*somehow*—help us catch a killer?"

The woman called Maggie—who had stood and stepped back to let the paramedics work—let out a gasp at Emilia's words. "Do you think Clifford is dead?"

"I'm afraid he is, ma'am," one of the paramedics said.

The other one covered the victim with a blanket as Maggie wailed and clutched her chest. Howard stepped over to the lady and spoke to her a moment.

Emilia faced one of the remaining uniformed cops. "Can you take all these people to the conference room and make sure they stay there?" She addressed the other one. "You guard the elevator and don't let anyone else in. Howard and I will be in the snack area with *Mr. I Don't Think We Need Fingerprints*. We'll call for the next witness when we're done with him. No one leaves the premises."

Howard called Emilia to his side and whispered, "The receptionist told me the man said 'Linc' as she cradled his head."

As Emilia mulled that over, Greta tapped her on the shoulder. "Can you tell me how you got here so fast? I hadn't even given the 911 operator the address and you were clearly already in the building since you had to check in with Danny downstairs. Was there already a call in to this location?"

"Why? Do you think someone heard something and called it in? We can look into that when we get back to the precinct. I'll make a note of it." Emilia put her firearm away and pulled out her notebook and pen. She flipped past the notes on the hooker case and started on a new page.

"If you weren't called here, why were you in the building?"

This woman Greta was trying Emilia's patience. Why was she so persistent in asking why they were there? That was suspicious in and of itself.

Before Emilia could think of a lie for why they were there since she really didn't want to tell this apparently too capable woman the real reason, Howard opened his mouth and blew her plan to keep it a secret.

"We were coming to interview your boss, Mr. Eisenger."

Greta raised an eyebrow. "About what?"

"Never mind. It doesn't matter." Emilia clapped her hands, thinking about the fact that the victim's last word was Linc. That wasn't something she planned to share with the man's right-hand woman. Better to confront him with it at an opportune time. "Everyone to the conference room except my first witness."

She smiled at the lawyer with the big mouth. The smile she knew she'd inherited from her grandfather. That one that would intimidate even an alligator. It was her game face.

❧❧❧

The street was blocked off when Lincoln tried to return to his office and, since it was after five, he decided to head home instead of trying to get past the barricades. A little curious about what was going on since it wasn't parade season or anything like that, he debated calling Greta to see what was up but ultimately decided against it. He couldn't bear to deal with her questions about how Myles was doing today.

A beer and a bowl of jambalaya was what he needed. Luckily, he'd made a batch over the weekend and all he'd have to do was reheat it when he got home. He'd also stocked up on Abita beer at the grocery store so he was set. There would be enough time to worry about work later.

Linc pulled into the driveway as his cell phone went off, playing the New Orleans Saints' fight song, the ringtone that told him that his legal assistant was calling. He rubbed the back of his neck and groaned before he picked it up. So much for winding down with a beer. Greta never called after hours unless it was an emergency and she was so competent that he knew her judgment would be sound if she chose to bother him after five.

He selected the answer icon. "Eisenger."

"Thank goodness I got you, Linc."

"What's wrong? I've been right here by my phone the entire trip back from Angola. Why are you so frantic?

You could've called before now."

"Actually, I couldn't. The police left the building in the last few minutes." Greta's words ended on a quaver.

"The police? What happened?" Dear God, was he going to have to go back into the office? Why didn't one of the other partners handle whatever was going on? Or was it one of his clients?

"Clifford Van Nuys is dead."

"Dead? What happened? He was fine when I left. I saw him on my way to Joe-Don's for a po-boy to go. Did he have a second heart attack? Why were the police called?"

"He was murdered."

"*Murdered?* Where? When?"

Lincoln could scarcely believe it. Yeah, the little man was a jerk but really? Who would want to murder him? He was harmless enough and had probably been a bully back when he was in school but those kinds of people usually ran from any real confrontation.

"In the office. Near the reception desk was where he died."

"In the *office*? Did they make an arrest?"

"No. There are two homicide detectives on the case. The man seems nice. The woman is a sarcastic little slip of a thing. I guess she has to be obnoxious to get any respect. She doesn't look like she could fight her way out of a vat of pudding. I have no idea why they promoted her to detective. I can't even really fathom how she passed the physical to be a cop. Don't they have height and weight requirements?"

"What are their names?" Linc couldn't figure out why Greta was so concerned about the female cop. Shouldn't she be focused on the dead law partner?

"She's Emilia Hammond and he's Howard Mills. I think we've had him as a witness on a case before. That one that took place over there by Mardi Gras World, remember?"

"Yeah, I remember him." Linc scratched his head. "Her name doesn't sound familiar—at least the Emilia part doesn't—but I remember there's a group of Hammonds in the NOPD. I bet she's related to them. Seems like there's a precinct captain named Emil Hammond."

"Maybe that's how she got a job in the first place."

"You really don't like this woman, do you?"

Greta sniffed. "No. I can't say I do. She's abrasive and rude. I can't wait for you to take her down a peg—" She paused. "—or twelve."

Linc glanced in his rearview mirror as something flashed. He recognized it as an undercover flashing light on the dashboard of a nondescript Ford sedan. "Looks like I'm going to meet the lady now."

"What do you mean?"

"I see a tall, skinny African-American man getting out of an undercover car in my driveway behind me. He's getting out on the driver's side and a very small woman who may also be part African-American with short, cropped hair is climbing out of the passenger side."

"That sounds like them. Call me back after you've taken her down a level or two. Eat her for dinner, boss."

"I confess I was looking forward to jambalaya, instead."

Linc hung up with Greta's laughter ringing in his ear.

Chapter 4

Howard knocked on the driver's side window of the silver Lexus sitting in the driveway of Lincoln Eisenger's house off St. Charles Avenue. He held his gun at the ready and Emilia had hers out as well. The car window slid down.

"What can I do for you, Detective Mills?" Linc asked.

"Come out of the vehicle with nothing in your hands and keep them where I can see them."

Howard opened the door and held his gun on Eisenger. Emilia moved to cover the area in front of the car and the driver's side.

Linc stepped out of the car with his hands in front of him. "You can't think I had anything to do with the death of Clifford Van Nuys."

"How did you even know about it if you shouldn't be a suspect?" Emilia asked.

"There's this device that someone was smart enough to invent. Maybe you've heard of it, ma'am. It's called a cell phone. All the employees at my firm have them and one of them happened to use hers to call me and tell me about my partner's death."

"Oh, ho, Howard, what we have here in front of us is a real smart-aleck. I can't wait to hear what he comes up with next. Should be a doozy after that brilliant remark." Emilia thought the man was arrogant but she imagined he had plenty of practice at it. Growing up in this area of the city tended to make people that way. Most of them that she'd met over the years made her hackles rise and this man was no different. So what if he was good-looking with that scruffy beard and loosened necktie? It was time to take him down. "Come inside the house, sir. We have some questions for you about your law partner."

"I don't believe I have to invite you inside my home and I don't believe you have the right to enter without my permission unless you have a warrant, Officer."

Linc looked Emilia up and down. His sneer only served to emphasize the difference in them. He had to be at least six feet, two inches and she was a mere four feet, ten inches in her bare feet.

Determined not to let his attitude deter her from her task, she shrugged. "Okay. Have it your way. Detective Mills and I will haul you on downtown to the precinct and chat with you there. Will you have someone to give you a lift back—if we don't arrest you, that is?"

Linc leaned his hip on the side of his car. "You have nothing on me, lady. You can't hang this on me. I wasn't even in this parish at the time the man died."

"How do you know? Do you have a time of death from the coroner? You could've left after he died for all we know."

She couldn't help herself. He seemed to bait her with every word. Why was she letting him get to her? This was the case she needed to prove herself on, and if she messed up because she let some moron of a Garden District lawyer get under her skin, she was lost already.

As soon as the thought formed itself in her head, she snorted. Yeah, she'd known some morons who'd passed the bar exam, but this man probably wasn't one of them.

"I'm sorry, Officer. I don't understand. I was told that the man was found dead in the lobby of our building sometime after lunch. I left with my own lunch to drive up to Angola to see my brother. We all know that trip up and back took most of the afternoon and, even if I hadn't spent any time at all with Myles, there's no way I was around the city to kill Van Nuys. You can check the records at Angola. It'll have my arrival time and my exit time. As you're aware, every visitor must sign in and out."

"Be sure we'll be checking, but it's still possible that you're involved," Emilia said. "We also know about the back entrance and how you're prone to come and go without checking in with security.

Linc crossed his arms and glared at her. "How do you figure that it's possible that I'm involved?"

"You and your brother are very clever. He's been convicted of murder himself—"

"Oh, so, in your esteemed opinion, the inclination to murder is something that's in the genes?" Linc took a step in Emilia's direction. "First of all, my brother was wrongfully convicted—*wrongfully*—and secondly, that's one of the most inane things I think I've ever heard in my life." Linc took another step toward her.

Emilia resisted the urge to back up, as she didn't want Eisenger to know he'd gotten to her and that she was a bit frightened by the anger in his voice. She threw a grateful glance at Howard as he took hold of Lincoln's upper arm.

"Hang on, man. No need to threaten the lady," Howard said.

"She's no lady and I didn't threaten her." Lincoln spread his arms and grinned but to Emilia it appeared to be more of a grimace than an actual smile. "I'm an innocent man standing in his own driveway being needled by an officer of the law. Maybe I need to make a call of my own to the police commissioner. Tell him all about the harassment I'm enduring based on the mere fact that I have a brother in Angola and I have a dead law partner who I couldn't possibly have had a chance to kill. What do you think?" Linc glared at Emilia. "How do you think that phone call could affect that gold shield that I bet you have had for about five minutes?"

"You don't have that kind of clout, mister. If you did, your brother wouldn't be in prison now, would he?"

At that comment, Lincoln did lunge at Emilia. She whipped her gun up and aimed it directly at his chest.

Howard stepped between them. "Put the gun down, Em. Right now. Put. It. Down."

She reluctantly placed her gun in the back waistband of her slacks. Who did he think he was, leaping at her like that? She wanted to take him down so bad, blood pounded in her ears. The vibrations were almost a physical pain. Why was he affecting her this way? She didn't usually rattle this easily. Maybe she was putting too much pressure on herself to solve this case in one day. The man was right. She really didn't deserve a gold shield if she was going to act stupid.

Glad that Howard was there and had stopped her from making a colossal mistake, she gritted her teeth and backed away from the Lexus. "Mr. Eisenger, we'll be back to discuss this matter further. Have a nice evening." She nodded her head at Howard. "Let's move out, Detective."

Lincoln barked out a laugh. "Have a nice evening? Really? That's all you've got after trying to murder me in my own driveway? That's rich."

Detective Mills held out his hand to shake Linc's. "No hard feelings, Eisenger?"

"You bet there are hard feelings, man. Take your rabid partner and get off my property. Don't come back unless you have a warrant in your hand or I'll be the one having someone arrested."

His eyes shot daggers across the driveway at Emilia. She barely refrained from dodging them as if they were real.

ⱥↄⱥↄ

As soon as the two officers left, Lincoln grabbed his phone, briefcase, and jacket from the car and headed to his porch. He debated whether to drive back down to his office area to check and see if the child prostitute was out there for the evening but decided that he really needed a night in and some rest from all the stress of the day. First, the hooker getting in his face about that cigarette, then the chat with Clifford, the trip to Angola and back, and now this murder. It was almost too much to process since everything had happened in such a short space of time. And the news about his brother risking his life in the prison rodeo was troublesome as well.

Something niggled at the back of his mind about that girl in the purple shorts and high-heeled boots but he couldn't figure out what it was. He shrugged and slid the key in the lock of his front door. He opened the etched-glass door, stepped inside, and let out a deep breath he hadn't even realized he was holding. Tossing his jacket and briefcase on the antique cherry wood hall tree that had belonged to his great-grandmother, Linc used the heel of his shoe to close the door behind him and turned toward the kitchen with his cell phone still in his left hand.

He placed the phone on the counter beside the stovetop and turned on the burner on his way to the refrigerator to retrieve his jambalaya to reheat. Before he could open the door to the appliance, the cell phone rang. This time it was the ringtone for his mother, an Elton John song about someone being back. Lincoln groaned and let the call go to voice mail. He certainly wasn't in the right frame of mind to deal with that woman.

Once his dinner was sufficiently warmed, Lincoln plated it and, grabbing a beer, sat at the high bar on the other side of the kitchen island from the cooktop. He dug in to the divine mixture of dirty rice, Andouille sausage, shredded chicken, and spices.

Before he'd taken two bites, the ringtone played again. His mother. Ignoring it, Linc kept eating. His gut clenched, as he knew the woman wouldn't stop calling until he answered but he was determined to pick up the phone on his own terms. Yes, this woman had given birth to him and his brother but there had never been any female on the planet who had less of a maternal instinct than she had. Lincoln had often thought that if they'd been born to Caroline in one of the poorer areas of the city that they would have ended up as wards of the state.

It wasn't so much that she abused them physically. It was more of an emotional thing or a case of being ignored until she needed or wanted something. Like now.

The third time the phone rang, Linc leaned over and grabbed it from where it sat near the pot on the stove. He answered right before the voicemail kicked in. "Hello, Mother."

"You've been ignoring me again, I see."

"It's the dinner hour and I know how sacred that is to you. I can only wonder at you breaking your own rule about using the phone at meal times. I was merely trying to follow that law that you pounded in my head as a kid and enjoy dining in peace, but since you kept ringing, I decided I had better pick up. What can I do for you to-day?"

"You could start with not being a smart-aleck but I know that's too much to ask."

"Please tell me the purpose of the call so I can get back to my meal." Linc sighed. He knew his mother would take as long as she needed on this call and he could complain all he wanted but he'd better not hang up.

"I heard Clifford Van Nuys is dead and that you're a suspect. What do you have to say about that? Your poor departed father would be absolutely broken hearted to learn that a second son has been found culpable in a murder case."

"First of all, *Mother*—" Linc stressed the word mother in such a way that she would have to know he was peeved at her. "—Dad would be distressed to know *one* son is in prison for a crime he didn't commit. And make no mistake, had Dad been alive when that happened, Myles would *not* have been convicted. And second—"

"Wait a minute there. Are you saying your father would have bribed that jury that convicted your brother?"

"Of course not. Dad was the most honest man I've ever known. What I'm saying is that Myles was set up and, if Dad were alive, he would've put all his resources to work to find out who really committed the crime and the right person would have been charged instead of being free on the streets to this day."

"Are you saying I didn't help your brother as much as I should have?"

"That's exactly what I'm saying."

Linc and his mother had this conversation on numerous occasions. He knew she was never going to concede that she was more interested in spending his father's money on her new husband's political campaigns than on saving her own son from prison. He was lucky it wasn't a death-penalty case because, sadly, his mother wouldn't have cared. She'd shown that by her actions.

"I didn't call you to talk about Myles."

Linc tapped the edge of his fork on his plate. "Then why did you call?"

"To let you know that I wasn't going to throw my money away on a defense lawyer for you. Both of my sons have grown up to disappoint me and be charged with murder. It makes me look bad as a parent. What happened to you two? You had the best life could offer and you both end up as killers."

Linc sat in stunned silence. When he found his voice, all he could think to say was, "Wow."

"Wow, what? I asked you a question. Wow is not a response." His mother's tone held the ice she usually reserved for speaking to her hired help who she treated as if they were servants from medieval times.

"Wow that you're such a cold-hearted witch is what wow means."

"How dare you disrespect me as your mother? You apologize right now."

"No. I won't. In fact, I'm going to be rude and hang up on you. Don't call back either as I won't be answering."

"Don't you dare hang up on me."

"I am. Bye, Mother." Linc turned off the phone and laughed.

He'd said he was going to hang up. Warned her twice even. Could that really count as hanging up on her? His legal mind told him no. His mother always told him how many things he did wrong and it amused him a little bit that he couldn't even be rude the right way.

He was not amused though that she thought he'd committed murder. What did that say about her as a mother and about him as a son? Giving up on figuring that out, he stood and stepped over to the sink to wash the dinner dishes. He'd never understand why the selfish woman ever *had* children. It was a mystery and he wished over and over again that he'd asked his father about. Now it was too late.

Chapter 5

You know it's Thursday night dinnertime at my folks' right?" Emilia asked Howard when they reached St. Charles Avenue. "We need to stop in for a few minutes, even if we can't eat, since you know how my mamma gets when one of her children fails to show up."

"We're entitled to a meal break. We've done all the interviews of the staff at the law office and that Joe-Don's po-boy is long gone. Your mother's pork chops and turnip greens would hit the spot about now. Call it in that we're headed to Algiers and will be off radio in a few minutes."

Howard turned their car toward the river to head across to Emilia's family home while she called in their break. "Now that you've met him, do you think that Ei-senger is dumb enough to kill his law partner right there on the premises?" he asked.

"You forget. I already met him when I was dressed as Amy the hooker. He didn't impress me then and he doesn't impress me now either."

"You're crazy, you know that, right?"

Emilia crossed her arms. "I don't know what you mean."

"You drew your gun on the man. You say he doesn't impress you but listen to this, Em, he has you now. You made a rookie mistake because you let that man get under your skin and now you're in a bit of a pickle."

"I still don't follow."

"The man has something on you that he can use to cause you issues on the force. He's now got the upper hand in this investigation. I don't really think he did the actual deed—he didn't get his own hands dirty—of that I'm sure. I'm positive he's smarter than that, but I *do* think he may have had a part in setting it up, based on what that Maggie woman said in her statement. I also don't like that there's a back entrance to that office where he can slip in and out at will without anyone knowing, and I can't wait to see those sign in sheets at Angola." Howard glanced over at Emilia. "But the fact of the matter is, he has the goods on you now and that could hamper this investigation."

Emilia ran her hands over her thighs to wipe the sweat that suddenly covered her palms. "Pfft. He's got nothing on me. You and I were the only people there. Who's going to believe him?"

Howard pulled the car over at the next business parking lot they came to. He turned off the engine and faced her full on.

"What? I thought you wanted a pork chop. Why'd you pull over?"

"I've got to say something and I want to look directly in your eyes to be sure my words go into that stubborn head of yours."

"Wow. What the heck? What are you so mad about?"

Emilia couldn't figure out what set Howard off but he sure was ticked about something. She knew his angry face almost as well as she knew her own.

"One of the things wrong with this city—and it has been wrong since time began so I'm not blaming *you* for it—is police corruption, and I can tell you right now, I'm not going to be part of it. I would hope that you wouldn't be either." He held his hand up. "Don't say anything yet. I can see that you want to, but let me finish first. I know you're putting a lot of pressure on yourself to solve not only that young prostitute's death but this new case that accidently landed in our laps. I am also quite sure that this pressure is about proving yourself to you grandfather, father, and brothers. Let me tell you, Em, they love you even if you don't become the most famous detective in the history of the NOPD."

"Do you think I was being corrupt?" Emilia was aghast at the idea.

"Sounded to me like you were suggesting I lie for you if that lawyer reported you for your actions."

"Sorry, I didn't mean for it to appear that way. I was merely pointing out we were the only ones there."

"That's where it starts, Em. Promise me that you will always be honest and, if Internal Affairs investigates you, that you'll tell them the truth."

"What do you believe *is* the truth?"

Howard smiled slightly. "That you let that rich white boy get under your skin and you reacted."

"Do you really think I would have shot him if you hadn't intervened?" Emilia was curious about his answer because she wasn't sure herself if she would have or not.

It was hard to move from patrol to homicide detective and transition to asking hard questions of suspects, as opposed to handling drunks or other minor calls. She liked to think she was making a smooth change but, most likely, she was blundering along, making a lot of mistakes. Thank God, they'd partnered her with the way-more experienced Detective Mills.

"I like to think you would have shaken yourself out of your anger before you shot the man but, to tell you the truth, I'm not so sure you would have. You've got to learn to rein in that temper. I would've thought your years on patrol would do that."

"Me, too. I think that they did but, for some reason, I'm letting myself get crazy about proving that it wasn't a mistake for me to get promoted. Being the youngest homicide detective in the city is daunting, in and of itself, but when you factor in that my entire family is NOPD, it makes it appear that I've been moved up the ladder as some kind of favor."

"All the more reason to be careful and thorough and not go off on a suspect then, isn't it?"

"Point taken. Now drive me to my mamma's so we can eat. We're using up our precious meal break with chatter and not food."

"Good point yourself Let's go eat." He cranked the engine, looked both ways, and, when it was clear, pulled out into traffic.

Emilia mulled over what he'd said as they drove. Howard was right. She was out of control and needed to rein herself in a notch.

e⁄sc⁄s

The sight of the house she'd grown up in always made Emilia happy—a two-story pale yellow clapboard with dark green shutters and a wide porch stretched across the front of the structure that exuded warmth. The white columns and railing made the place look comfortable and homey. A set of four white wicker chairs and a table sat at one corner. On the other side were a couple of rocking chairs. Many happy days were spent on those chairs, watching the neighbors pass by and wasting time in the summer months hanging out with friends. Her brothers also used to entertain the community with their jazz music as teens before they formed their real band as adults and played some nights in the French Quarter, after they got off duty with the NOPD.

Emilia and Howard entered the house through the front door. As soon as they were over the threshold, Emilia sniffed the air. "Ahh, nothing smells as good as my mother's home-cooking."

"You're right about that." Her father, Douglas, came into the foyer from the living room. "I can almost taste that fried chicken now. You know the taste buds are closely related to the sense of smell." He rubbed his hands together.

"You and your theories about food, Doug." Howard held his hand out and shook her dad's. "But what about the pork chops? I thought Dorothea was cooking chops."

"Don't you fret, Howard. I heard you were coming and I fried a few chops, too. I know how you love them." Dorothea exited the kitchen, wiping her hands on her apron. "Once my other two police force kids get their rears here, we'll dig in."

"Don't forget Granddad. He's going to be here, right?" Emilia asked.

"I don't think so. I heard they had some kind of issue up near his precinct and he's probably tied up with that still. I'm lucky mine is a few blocks closer to civilization than his. I was able to get off right on time. Lord knows I like to get home while dinner is still hot." Douglas patted his stomach. "I wish those boys of mine would get here so we could eat."

The front door banged open and Emilia's brothers, Jacob and Raymond, came in.

"Hey, Momma, I can smell that food all the way out-side. Let's eat," Raymond said as he ran the palm of his hand over his short-cut afro.

Dorothea laughed. "Son, you need to greet your mother in a nicer way than that."

Raymond planted a kiss on his mother's cheek. "I figured that you would appreciate a hungry child who loves your food."

Jacob made a face at his sister. "Ooh, look, it's New Orleans' latest detective. I can't believe she found time to eat with her lowly brothers."

Emilia knew he wasn't kidding around. They were only a year apart and he was the elder of the two. She was aware that it stuck in his craw that she made detective before he did. He hadn't made a secret of his feelings, and she'd kind of avoided the Thursday dinners since her promotion. But her mother begged her to try to come and to understand what Jacob was experiencing. Emilia wouldn't be surprised if he wanted her to fail on her first cases.

"Stop it, Jacob. This is a family dinner and no one is going to be ugly to anyone at my table. Come on in and sit down. It's all on the table except the meat." Dorothea smiled at Howard. "Bring your too-skinny self in the kitchen and help me get the meat on the platter."

Emilia, her brothers, and her father moved to the dining room and took their assigned seats. In a few moments, her mother and partner came in with a plate of chicken and pork piled high. They were laughing.

"What's so funny?" Emilia asked.

"Howard was telling me about your day." Dorothea sat and nodded to the empty spot on the table. "Put the platter there."

"What about my day?"

Emilia knew she was being paranoid but what was enjoyable about the day they'd had? Surely, there was nothing amusing about it. No way would Howard betray her and tell her mother about Emilia pulling her gun on a suspect, would he? And that wasn't funny, anyway.

Dorothea picked up the bowl of mashed potatoes and passed them to her right. "Nothing really about the day itself. More like the outfit you've been wearing when you're investigating that poor girl's death."

"That outfit is pretty hideous, but I'm sad for the girls. I sure feel sorry for those ladies who live that life. It's got to be horrific and I don't mean only the fact that they wear some awful clothing." Emilia snagged a piece of chicken and cut it open to let the steam escape. The smell of the crispy crust wafted into her nose. Pure bliss.

"What's it look like?" Raymond asked.

"Let's just say it has purple short shorts that almost show Em's cheeks and also a red curly wig for her head.

A red so red that the clown from that restaurant looks blonde by comparison." Howard speared a bite of pork chop and put it in his mouth.

"Lord, you gotta take a picture of that. We need it for the annual Christmas card," Jacob said.

"Very funny." Emilia wanted to smack her brother but that was nothing new. They'd spent their lives bickering and arguing. Being so close in age, she knew they always would.

Jacob smirked. "I bet it is. Funny, that is."

Before she could respond to his taunt, her cell phone rang. She answered it. "Detective Hammond."

Jacob made a face that Emilia could see from the corner of her eye. Yep, he was jealous. There wasn't a darn thing she could do about it, though. He'd make rank one day and then all would be well again. While she was on the phone, she noticed Howard eating fast. He had to know it was dispatch on the phone. Dinner break was over.

As soon as she disconnected the call, she said, "Sorry all. We have to go." She wiped her mouth and stood. Placing her napkin on the table, she turned to her mother. "Thanks for dinner. I wish I could've eaten more but sadly, we have another hooker who was attacked."

"Do they not have any other detectives in your precinct but you and Mills here?" Raymond asked.

"Sure they do but since we're the investigating officers on the prostitute's death and this new one was attacked in the same area, and we're still on duty because of the Van Nuys murder, they're calling us in off our break to go down and talk to the witnesses."

"Did dispatch say this one is still alive?" Howard asked.

"Yeah. She's in a coma though." Emilia smiled at her mom. "Sorry. We need to get back to the other side of the river."

"Let me wrap you some chicken. It'll only take a second." Dorothea was already moving to the kitchen with the platter of meat."

"Save some for us, Mom," Raymond and Jacob said at the same time.

Emilia shook her head and grinned at her dad. "I hope the growing boys leave some for you."

"The heck with me. They had better leave some for their granddad. He'll be starving when he gets here. He's a big man with a big appetite as you know." Her dad smiled. "Go on now and make us proud."

She followed Howard out to the porch where her mother stood with a foil wrapped package and two soft drinks in cans. "Here. Eat this on the way back over the bridge."

"Thanks, Mom." Emilia kissed her mother on the cheek and made her way to the passenger side of the car. She opened the door and slipped inside. "At least we got a snack."

"I don't know why you worry about them being

proud of you, Em. They clearly already are. It seems to me that you could let go of a little bit of that pressure you're placing on yourself on their behalf."

"Maybe you're right. I'll think about it if I ever get any spare time."

"Good luck with that." Howard cranked the car and backed out of the Algiers house's driveway.

Chapter 6

Linc tried to watch the news but all the coverage about Clifford Van Nuys made him sick to his stomach. True, he hadn't cared for the man but he didn't want him dead. All the talk about the Eisenger law firm led the newscasters to mention Myles, and the more Linc thought about the visit he'd had from law enforcement, the more it seemed as if a noose were being tightened around his own neck. The television anchors also seemed to want to glorify the person that Van Nuys had been. Since Linc knew the man was smarmy and a jerk, it was a little hard to swallow all the praise directed at the dead man.

Giving up on the newscast, Linc opened a novel he'd started reading the day before but his mind couldn't settle on it either. The more he thought about it, the more he realized he couldn't sit by and let one more night go by with that poor girl out on the streets being the victim of another pervert. Why this particular girl was under his skin, he still didn't know. What he *did* know was that she was out there and he was inside in his comfortable environment, safe and secure. He couldn't stand it. He recognized he was restless and antsy after his rough day, and his mind wandering to the hooker and her plight was a way to take his mind off the hours since lunch.

Throwing the book aside, Linc slid his shoes back on and grabbed his phone and keys. He was going back to the office building and would scour the area for the girl. He'd take the fake cigarettes again and maybe she'd see him littering and come bless him out again. As soon as she did, he would talk her into letting him help her, even if he had to promise to pay the girl the rate the pimp expected her to earn during the time. That was crazy he knew but he had to convince her to let him help her get off the streets.

Out in the Lexus, he placed his phone in the cup holder and turned off the radio. He sure didn't want to hear any more news about Clifford Van Nuys today. He backed out of the driveway and headed toward his office.

It was still early on a Thursday night and a lot of people were out for dinner and, of course, drinking and dancing. New Orleans was definitely a party town and the office building owned by the Eisenger firm since the mid-1800s was close to the French Quarter so there was always a crowd in the area. The private parking lot, hidden off street, was a godsend and Linc was thankful, as always, that his family trust owned the building and lot. He parked in his normal spot and got out of the car.

Deciding not to enter his building via the back door but to walk the long way around, Linc ambled along on watchful alert to, hopefully, find the girl. He saw several prostitutes walking down the sidewalk but none of the ones who appeared to be underage. He knew the adult women may need help as well but he was focused on assisting those whom he sensed didn't have a choice in what they were doing. It was a fact of life he'd learned early on that some women chose that lifestyle as a career path.

After a couple of hours of popping in to various bars and cafes, Linc decided that the girl was holed up somewhere and that he should head home since he did have to work the next day. He had a hearing set in federal court and thought he should probably read over the file ahead of time. He turned the corner leading to the parking lot.

Ahead of him was a person in purple short shorts and a red wig. Could this be her? He increased his pace to try to catch up to the girl so he could see her face.

He jogged along, narrowing the distance between them. His loafers weren't the best to make haste in since the soles had no traction to speak of. Linc skidded in a couple of places where there was litter on the ground but he remained upright.

In the moment before he could've reached out and touched her, a tall blonde-haired woman stepped into his path. "As I live and breathe, it's Lincoln Eisenger down here after work hours seemingly chasing some hooker. Have you fallen that far down into the pits of depression since we broke up, Lincoln dear?"

Of all the luck to run into Mary Lou Stratton. Cripes. Could this day *get* any worse? What gods had he angered for so much to go wrong in one twenty-four hour period? This was not good. Besides the fact that his prey had escaped, now he'd have to make nice with the ex-girlfriend.

Linc pasted on a smile. "How are you, Mary Lou?"

"Obviously better than you." She turned to the man who stood at her side. "I have a date and don't need to chase prostitutes. Do you know Buckingham Prevatte?"

"Yes, I know Buck." Linc shook the man's hand. Better that poor sucker be attached to the barracuda than him. "What brings you to town?"

"I'm visiting Mary Lou for the weekend. I came today. Took tomorrow off. She invited me over when she stayed in Baton Rouge with me last weekend."

"You two an item, then?"

"Don't be jealous, Lincoln dear. You know you're still important to me." Mary Lou always called him Lincoln dear and it still annoyed him as much as it did when they were dating.

"I'm so *not* jealous, Mary Lou, that I wish the best for you and ole Buck here. I hope you make him as happy in your relationship as you made me the day you broke up with me."

Mary Lou simpered and smiled but, as Linc watched her face, it became crystal clear when she understood exactly what he'd said. Her face fell and she reached out as if to smack his face.

Linc caught her wrist in his left hand before she made contact with his skin. "Now, now, dear Mary Lou, you don't want to do that."

She huffed and pouted. "You're an awful bastard and I can't stand you."

"All the more reason for us both to be glad you saw me for who I really am and banished me from your side. It was what I deserved and I hope Buck here gets to stay with you for as long as he desires." Linc bowed. "Now, if you'll excuse me, I have things to do."

"Like pick up a lady of the night?" Mary Lou's voice dripped sarcasm.

"At least a lady of the night is honest about what she is." Linc turned and went back the same direction from whence he'd come. He could hear Mary Lou spluttering behind him. He didn't care. Even before she called off their relationship, it had become clear to him that she was all about the Eisenger money.

He walked down the sidewalk, full of remorse that he hadn't been able to catch the girl in the purple shorts. So much for saving her tonight. He hoped she found a safe place to stay, instead of turning a trick. Linc decided he'd have to try again the next night since this day needed to end, and end now, before anything else went wrong.

എൟൟ

Friday morning was drizzly and overcast. Emilia stretched out in her bed and wiggled her toes. It had been a long day and night the evening before but she and Howard had made a little bit of progress on the prostitute case. The latest victim was in a coma but one of the other girls had seen a pale blue or silver Volvo in the area before the victim was found. The car had been moving slowly down the road and had stopped a few times to chat to some of the ladies strolling the streets.

The witness gave a good description of the driver. It was a white man with a deep voice and, as she said, "a Southern-man accent." Emilia had a general idea of what that meant but she knew they were more likely to find the man based on what the witness called his head of gray hair that was thick, straight, and lush. The girl had been working with Howard and the sketch artist when Emilia went back on the streets for another hour before she decided she needed to go home and get some rest.

Now she was awake and needed to get back to the precinct to see what was going on. Time to get up and at it. She tossed her thin blanket aside, rose, and took a quick shower.

A knock at the door as she dressed startled her. "Who's there?"

"It's your breakfast."

"I'm not sure I want to eat any breakfast that can talk

to me through walls," Emilia called out as she moved to open her door.

She knew exactly who it was, of course. It was Alyce-Faye, her best friend. Emilia flung the door open to find her pal standing there with a bag from Café Du Monde. She also was trying her best not to drop two paper cups. Emilia knew her own would have chicory and be black and strong. Her more timid mate would have ordered herself some chocolate milk.

"Let me help you before you spill that liquid caffeine that I need more today than I've needed in a long time." Emilia took one of the cups from Alyce-Faye. "You're up early."

Alyce-Faye waggled the bag. "Here's some sugar to help jump-start your day, too."

"I'm actually in a big hurry today. Not only do I have two murders to investigate, there's also the beating of another prostitute we're pretty sure is connected."

"You still have to eat."

"I know and I appreciate you bringing beignets by— since that's all Du Monde serves—I feel safe in saying that's what's in the bag." Emilia held her hands out. "Give me one to go."

"Sit down for like one minute. I have something to share that might help you and Howard. You've worked too hard since you got promoted. Surely the department can spare you for ten minutes to eat something before you have to head out and start kicking people in the rear."

"Fine. I guess I have been a little obsessive lately, but please don't tell me you've read my cards and therefore know the identity of the murderer. I'd have a hard time convincing my captain that we need to make an arrest based on my friend's Tarot set." Emilia sat at her table in the corner of the one room apartment she rented over a jewelry shop in the French Quarter.

Alyce-Faye took two white fluted-edge stoneware plates from Emilia's red-painted cabinets and sat with the bag of beignets. She dug them out and placed three on each of their plates. "Now, eat while I tell you about what I learned."

Emilia looked at her friend over the top of the coffee cup as she sipped. Alyce-Faye was a Catholic-school-educated girl who had changed her look completely. She wore her hair long and it flowed down her back in loose curls. The blonde in her hair was brighter than when she was in school, and she also had several strands colored in various shades of pink and blue, as well as lavender. She sported a white leotard and a long skirt that was made of tulle. And the colors matched her hair. This was her costume for the French Quarter where she read Tarot cards and palms under the trees on the sidewalk in front of St. Louis Cathedral. The bells on her sandals tinkled as she swung her legs under the table.

"Tell me your source first." Emilia had out her notebook ready to jot down Alyce-Faye's information. The area near the cathedral was a center of gossip so it was very likely that her information would be a lead of some sort.

"You know the guy who stands near Pirates Alley and paints himself gold?"

"Yeah. Adam Pipersburg, right?"

"Oh, you *do* know him?"

"Of course. I walked a beat for a few years, you know." Emilia took a big bite of one of the beignets. Powdered sugar went everywhere.

"You never *walked* a beat, crazy. You were in a squad car."

"I *did* have to get out of it on occasion, you know. Patrol squads don't just run around wasting fuel."

"Humpf. Could've fooled me. I've needed one on more than one occasion and they ignored me—one guy even refused to take my statement once because he said I should've seen that pick-pocket coming since supposedly I can tell the future."

"That's the oldest and most stupid joke in the world. I hope you reported him for refusing." Emilia ate another beignet.

"His partner was nicer and took my statement so I let it go."

Emilia wiped her hands on the thighs of her jeans and picked up her pen. "Tell me what Adam said to you."

"He saw that girl who got hurt in Pirates Alley. She was there about two hours before she was found beaten up."

"What was she doing? I mean, what was she doing in the alley that would cause him to think something was amiss?"

"He said she was arguing with someone and that person slapped her in the face. She then turned to walk away and the person grabbed her arm and twisted it behind her back until she looked at the person again."

"Did he recognize the guy who did it? Did he say he could make a good identification? We have a sketch artist drawing a likeness of a man that one of the other girls saw. Do you think if I took this over to the gold man, that he would be able to say if it was the same person?"

"I'm not sure. He said the person had her head covered with a scarf or something like that."

Emilia glanced up from the note pad. "*Her*?"

"Yep. He said it was a woman. Or what he thought was a woman—you know as well as I do that there is a huge population of transvestites, transgenders, and plain ole cross-dressers in this city. It could've been anyone really." Alyce-Faye nodded. "Yep, could be anybody."

"Super. Now what? Maybe I *do* need a Tarot reading, after all."

Chapter 7

The weekend came fast and seemed to pass even faster. Linc had no luck on either Friday or Saturday nights in his quest to find the underage hooker.

Not wanting to give up the search, he knew he'd have to skip the Sunday night trip to the French Quarter to look for her, nevertheless. But every day that went by caused his anxiety to rise. He was sure that she might have become the latest victim of whomever was preying on the young girls in the Quarter. He'd heard one was in a coma in the hospital and was afraid it was her since he hadn't seen her on either Friday or Saturday night.

As well as being in a stew over the prostitute and Myles's riding in the rodeo, those two detectives were still trying to get him to come in and have a sit down chat with them. There was no way was he going to do that. He knew better than to try to have a discussion with law enforcement once they'd decided who their suspect was going to be. Sadly, Myles hadn't followed that rule and look where he ended up. Myles made the mistake of thinking he could handle an interrogation since he was innocent, but that sure hadn't worked out for him. Lincoln wasn't going to let somebody trap him into saying anything that could be misconstrued or twisted into something it wasn't.

Linc had nothing to hide but in his years as a lawyer, he'd seen it all. Some folks confessed when they didn't intend to because they were either sleep-deprived or had to use the facilities and the cops made promises of food, sleep or whatever the person needed if he'd merely "tell the truth". Some folks became so desperate that they'd say what the cops wanted to hear. Not him. He wasn't saying a word and he wasn't going to their territory. It was too much like going in the lion's den.

On Sunday morning, after a quick breakfast of a bacon, egg and cheese biscuit, and a glass of orange juice, Linc, in his jeans and polo shirt, got into his Lexus and headed up to Angola prison. He could scarce believe he was going to see his brother in a rodeo. The brother who'd never even wanted to wear dungarees as a kid was going to actually get down and dirty in an arena full of livestock. He guessed he was happy that Myles had found an activity he liked in order to the pass the time but Linc couldn't help but wish he was going to a dressage show and Myles was free and out of prison.

Putting aside his depression at his brother's fate, Linc drove on until he got to the prison near the Mississippi line. Pulling into a parking space, he was surprised to see several people he knew from New Orleans walking past his car on their way to the entrance gates. Who knew this was such a popular destination on an October Sunday afternoon?

Anticipating that he wouldn't get to see his brother other than on the actual floor of the arena, Lincoln stepped toward the ticket taker's booth prepared to go in and find his seat. He figured he'd be subjected to a search but when he got to the front of the line, he was surprised when the officer on duty said he needed to take his phone back to his car since they didn't allow any cameras or recording devices on the rodeo grounds and that would include his phone.

On his way to lock the phone in his Lexus, Linc spotted his mother and her new husband across the parking lot. He ducked his head down and hoped she wouldn't notice him. What the heck was she doing here? She was completely *not* a rodeo kind of woman. There must be some kind of political interest for her husband to be here.

They walked on to the gate and didn't seem to see him. He hoped his seat wouldn't be near theirs.

Phone stowed in the trunk, Linc headed to the gate again. He passed inspection this time around and was let in to the facility. He made his way to his assigned seat and scoped out the area around him to see if his mother was anywhere close.

He turned around and saw a few more people he knew. Deciding to go over and chat with them, Linc walked down the few levels to where they stood. "Hey, Blake and Jennifer. This is my first time for the rodeo. Have you come before?"

"We come every year. You need to go down and check out all the cool things the inmates make and sell. They have some leather work items as well as lamps and things like that." Jennifer smiled. "I love collecting from this one guy. Look at what I got this year." She lifted her shirt to show a thin brown belt with an intricate design carved in it.

"I'd like to see what they have. How do I get to where they are?" Linc asked.

"Come on. We'll show you. The first part of the rodeo starts in twenty minutes but you have time to look around a few moments, anyway." Jennifer led Linc and Blake out of the tiers and down to the area set aside for the inmates to sell their wares.

"This is impressive," Linc said.

"Isn't it? The warden came up with the idea. It helps morale for the men to have something to do all year and then sell what they make here on the rodeo weekends. It seems to have cut down on rioting and has also given some of the men a new skill that they can use on the outside when they're paroled or their sentences are served."

Blake pointed across from where they stood. "That guy over there is the one Jennifer likes to buy from. Want to see what he has?"

"Sure. Why not?" Linc was even more impressed with the place after he'd looked over some of the items for sale. This warden really did have the inmates' best interests at heart.

Maybe Myles would be okay here, after all, if the appeals didn't work and if no additional evidence was discovered to get him a new trial. At least he wasn't somewhere that would crush his soul completely.

An announcer came on the overhead microphone. "The first event will start in five minutes. Please take your seats."

Linc shook hands with his friends. "I'll see you all later. Want to grab a drink before heading back to the city after the rodeo is over?"

"Sure. Sounds good. See you then," Blake said. They made their way to their seats.

A local television news anchor came out to the middle of the field and stood at attention. In a few moments, the announcer asked everyone to stand for the national anthem. A group of men walked out and stood behind the celebrity. They all removed their hats and placed them over their hearts. Linc recognized his brother on the second row.

A recording of the music came on and the anchorman sang the national anthem. When the song was over, while the audience clapped and whistled, the men tossed their hats in the air and whooped and hollered.

It was show time.

෴

"I can't believe that we're up here at the Louisiana State Penitentiary on a rodeo day. What were we thinking?" Emilia asked Howard. They sat in a traffic jam on the highway near the prison.

"You know we gotta follow the leads. That guy your friend knows that dresses in gold paint led us here on a rodeo day, partner, so here we are."

Emilia crossed her arms. "I still don't think this is going to help us at all."

"It's worth a try. We know it's a long shot but he *did* identify that drawing. He thinks it's a guy who he's seen at the rodeo in some official capacity. So, we mill around behind the scenes and see if we can find this dude and then we question him about the girls. If we solve that case, it'll free us up to solve the Van Nuys murder. You do agree that we need to get one of them out of the way so we can focus on the other, right?"

"I totally agree. I'm worn out is all. We've been on our feet it seems like all day and night for the last sixty hours. I've been in my clothes and then in Amy's so many times, I'm afraid if too many more days go by that I'll be wearing her wig with my jeans and jacket or her purple shorts with my sneakers. I never know from one second to the next who I am and what I'm wearing."

"Let's get there and parked and then, hopefully, we can get you back to one set of clothes. I'm sure I don't need to ask which you'd rather live your life in, do I?"

"No. You sure don't. I'm a no fuss kind of girl. All that makeup Amy wears makes my face itch."

"It looks good on you." Howard snickered.

"Yeah right. Never mind that." She glanced around the parking lot. "I don't know why this has to be so difficult. Why do we have to drive all the way up here to see if we can find some guy that drives a silver Volvo, or maybe a light blue one, who may or may not have anything to do with our case. Seems a bit like a dog chasing his tail."

"You really need an attitude adjustment, girl."

Emilia sighed. "I know. I must be the most unlikable person in the world. I don't know how you put up with me."

Howard laughed. "Not the world. Just the NOPD."

Emilia giggled. "Thanks. I think."

"You forget, I know the real you. The one you try to keep hidden. The one that loves puppy dogs and romance novels."

"You know I've never read a romance novel in my life." Emilia punched Howard on the shoulder. "I do confess to a love of the little fellas with wet noses, though."

"Ahh. So, in order to get you to date him all a guy needs is a wet nose?"

"Very funny. You know I gave up on men after that loser you and Detective Smith set me up with—you remember him, right? The one who meowed at me after he tried to massage my feet when we went back to my place after dinner? He was a real charmer."

Howard snorted. "You'll never forgive us for that, will you? How were we to know? He seemed perfectly normal when we met him."

"He was a lunatic for sure. I'll probably die an old maid since I've arrested almost every good-looking man in New Orleans, and the ones I haven't arrested think I'm too abrasive. They can't take me home to meet their mammas since I'm a smart mouthed, obnoxious street cop. I have no manners."

"You're not *that* bad. I *have* seen you be kind to people. You might have to try harder than me to be loveable but you can do it. I have faith in you. Besides, you have many friends and are as loyal to them as they are to you. You must have something going for you. The right man—the one who can tame you—hasn't come along."

"I'm twenty-eight, you're thirty-five. You sure you're more charming than me? You've got a few years on me and I don't see a Mrs. Mills at home waiting for your handsome rear to prance through the door."

"Thanks for admitting my rear is handsome but I have to set you straight on one thing."

"What's that?"

He laughed and pulled into a parking space. "Howard Mills doesn't prance."

"Yes, you do. Especially when there's a pretty girl around."

Howard turned the key to shut off the engine and faced her. "That's really wrong because, if that's true, I'd be prancing all day with the pretty girl I have as a partner—and I don't mean Amy."

"That's sweet, but you're so full of malarkey, I'm going to ignore you. Let's go. We need to let the warden know we're here and out of our jurisdiction in case we need assistance." Emilia opened her car door and stepped out of the vehicle.

They made their way to the entrance of the prison to check in as law enforcement so they could enter the rodeo area with special passes and with their firearms.

Once inside the facility and with their badges prominently displayed, Emilia and Howard wandered around the paddock areas where the animals were being held. Their tipster had indicated that he thought the man with the thick gray hair and the Volvo was a stable owner or backer. The informant also thought the man would be with the livestock during the event.

Searching the area over the noise of what was going on out in the arena was tedious. The sound of the crowd yelling and cheering seemed to reverberate all around them.

When Emilia had almost decided that she'd been right about the waste of time it was to drive all the way up to Angola, out of the corner of her eye, she caught a glimpse of a tall man with a thick mass of gray hair on his head. He was moving toward the fence around the bottom of the arena as if he were going to observe whatever activity was going on.

"Over there." Emilia poked Howard in the side and pointed at the man's retreating back,

"Let's go." Howard led the way and in a few moments, they caught up with the guy when he stopped to lean on the fence.

Emilia glanced out at the action and gasped.

"What?" Both the man and Howard asked at the same time.

"That rodeo clown over there flagging down that bull is Lincoln Eisenger. What's he doing in this rodeo?"

Chapter 8

Linc watched from the stands as the rodeo started. His brother came out dressed in baggy britches tied at the waist with a rope. He also had on a stars and stripes patterned red, white, and blue shirt and a huge red cowboy hat. Myles had some white paint under each eye in the shape of a half-moon and a white paint patch on his chin as well. His nose was painted red. He looked happy and Linc knew he had a smile on his own face that matched his brother's.

Not being familiar with rodeos and the people who performed in them, Linc was interested to see what would happen next.

The men with his brother stood to each side of a chute where a bull was penned in. The animal was shaking his head and snorting. This was kind of scary. What was Myles expected to do?

He turned to the lady beside him who'd been cheering off and on through the first part of the events. "What are they doing?"

"They're getting ready to put a rider on that bull and let him out. The clowns are there to distract the bull when the rider falls off so the bull doesn't gore him."

"So you're pretty sure that the rider is going to fall off?"

"Oh, yeah, honey. Those are some mean critters and they don't want that rider on their back. The contest is in how long the cowboy can keep his seat."

"Isn't it dangerous for the clowns then? Won't the bull want to find someone to target?"

"Sure enough. That's a pretty dangerous job out there, mister. I can tell you I've known some adrenaline junkies who love taunting that bull and getting too close to it in order to risk their own safety."

Linc's gut bottomed out. Was Myles going to do the same thing? Did he see this as his way to get out of prison in such a way that he wouldn't be taking his own life but would be hurt or killed in an accident? Surely not. He'd appeared way too happy at finding something to keep himself busy when Linc had seen him on Thursday. This couldn't be suicide by bull.

"Thanks for explaining it to me. I've never been to a rodeo before."

"Ahh, nice. First timer. You'll enjoy it. Do you have an inmate you're looking for or did you just decide to head to a rodeo this fine fall day?"

"That clown down there in the stars shirt is my brother." Linc pointed down to the spot where Myles stood and realized that the rider was in place and the gate on the chute was in the process of lifting. It took all the strength he had not to grab the woman's arm and clench it in fear.

"You seem pretty nervous. I can tell you that they made darned sure that he's trained before they let him down there in that arena. Watch. He'll be fine."

The bull ran out in to the center of the arena bucking the man on his back. When the guy hit the ground in a few seconds, the bull kept running. He made a beeline for Myles.

Linc didn't even realize he was on his feet until the woman beside him leapt to her feet as well. It seemed as if the whole world was standing and rooting either for the bull to take down Myles or vice versa. The roar of the crowd was intense and echoed off the walls and floors of the arena as Myles darted to the side, and the other two clowns yelled at the bull and tossed some flags at him to get his attention.

About the time Linc decided that his heart would explode if they didn't do something, the biggest clown ran straight in front of the bull and, using a steel barrel, ducked down inside it. The bull hit the barrel and stunned himself. As the animal reeled back from the barrel, two other men leapt from the safety of the sidelines, got the bull in hand, and led him off.

The rider as well as the three clowns bowed to the audience. Linc wiped his brow while the audience clapped and cat-called.

After they were seated, Linc smiled at the lady beside him. "Pretty darned stressful. I don't know how people stand it. I thought my heart would burst out of my chest and land throbbing at my feet."

"See?" She grinned. "That's the fun part. If your adrenaline was that high up here in the safety of the stands, imagine how those guys down there feel. They can actually smell that nasty bull and his hot breath on their necks."

Linc laughed. "You know, this is worse than car racing for making me nervous."

"Why does that make you nervous?"

"The sound of the motors whirring around and around and then the crashes. It seems to make my heart rate go up too fast as well."

"You might want to get that ticker of yours checked, son. You seem too young to be having all these cardiac issues." The woman cackled a laugh. "Look. Time for the next rider. There's your brother again. Do you need me to hold your hand? Or maybe one of my friends over here beside me?"

Linc glanced over at the line of four women who were all at least in their sixties. They all waved at him and smiled. One of them called out, "Come on over here, sugar. We'll take care of you."

"Thanks. I appreciate it. If I fall out over here, call an ambulance." Linc laughed then focused his attention back on the action. This time his brother didn't get in the same kind of trouble as the first round.

After watching several more rounds of competitors, Linc was beginning to relax. Maybe this was a pretty safe sport after all.

The next competitor spent less than two seconds on the bull. The huge animal turned quickly and dipped his head down. He stomped his foot in the dirt and the dry dust went flying. One of the rodeo clowns stopped and wiped his eyes as if the dirt was blocking his vision. Before Myles or the third clown could get to the bull to distract it, the bull ran at the felled rider and gored him in the side with his horn. The man fell to the ground and slumped over.

Chaos broke loose on the field and guards as well as cowboys covered the floor of the arena. The cowboys herded the bull off to the livestock area and the guards cleared a path for the ambulance that had been on standby in the pits.

The announcer came on. "Everyone keep your seats. The rider is still alive and we need to get him out of here and to the hospital. We promise to start back up in a few minutes. We'll be moving on to the calf-roping event next so keep your seats and hang on for a little while. There will be some popcorn and peanut salesmen coming around. Please remain seated."

Linc turned to the lady beside him. "Wow. How often does this kind of thing happen?"

"Not as often as you might imagine. It's rare."

"I tell you what. I wish my brother would pick something safer to keep him occupied while he serves his sentence. I think that guy down there who sells leather belts may need an apprentice."

"You're pretty funny. Now that your brother's got a taste of this life, he's not going to be satisfied tanning leather."

"I'm going to do my best to talk him into it, though."

"Good luck with that, dear." The woman patted his thigh. "By the way, I'm Patsy. My bunco playing friends and I come every weekend in October to see this. There's also a date in April. We'd love to have you be our seatmate next week, too. We're having a ball watching your reactions to all that's going on."

"I'm happy to be your amusement, Patsy. I don't know what bunco is but I bet you all have a great time with it. You seem to be a fun-loving group."

"You live up this way?"

"No. I live in New Orleans." Linc held his hand out. "I'm Lincoln Eisenger."

Patsy shook it. "Sometime when you're up this way visiting your brother, give me a call and we'll teach you to play bunco. It's a dice game."

"I'll do you one better." Linc pulled his wallet out of his pocket and extracted one of his business cards. He handed it to her. "Call me when you ladies want to come down to my city. I'll take you to dinner and we can play this dice game at my house."

"You want us old biddies to come a-calling?" Patsy stared down at the card. "Why would a fancy big-time lawyer like you want to hang out with a bunch of old ladies? You got no girlfriend? Wife?"

"Nope." Linc shook his head. "I have no women in my life. I think it's time I found some who know how to have fun, don't you?"

The lady blushed. "You mean us?"

"I do indeed. I can't believe how friendly and open you all are. As I sat here today all alone and worried about my brother, you took note and made me feel better about the whole thing. It's a gift, my new friend, and I'm grateful."

"That's sweet. I think we'll take you up on the invitation. You may regret it, though."

"No. I don't think so, Patsy. I think we're going to be pals and I can't wait to learn to play bunco. I hope no broncos are involved because I am *not* getting on a bull."

"I promise not to make you do that." Patsy's laughter almost drowned out the announcer's news that the rodeo was about to recommence. Almost but not quite.

಄಄಄

"Don't be silly, Em. That's Lincoln Eisenger's

brother Myles. The newspapers always said the two of them could be twins and touted them as the two most eligible men in the Garden District as well as the handsomest. They had it all. Looks, charm, and money. They *do* look a lot alike. It's the hat and the paint on Myles's face that's throwing you off. It's covering up his most likely shorter hair and cleaner shaven face. It's an easy mistake to make."

"It sure startled me for a second." Emilia turned to the gray-haired man beside them. She held out her hand. "I'm Detective Emilia Hammond and this is my partner, Howard Mills. We're New Orleans police and would like to ask you a few questions."

"What's this about? I'm kind of busy. Those are my bulls out there and I need to be focused on them at the moment." The man practically snarled the words.

"This really can't wait," Emilia said.

"It's going to have to, missy."

Determined not to let the man get under her skin, Emilia smiled through her gritted teeth. "Really, it's a few quick questions."

"I've been around cops, lady, and I know better than that. Tell you what, let me pay attention to this part of the rodeo and once the bull riding is over, I'll even buy you a hot chocolate and we can chat then. How's that sound?"

Howard intervened and Emilia knew it was because he thought she was going to lose it, since this man was so patronizing. She wasn't, though. She knew this kind of guy tried to push buttons in order to gain an advantage. Emilia wasn't going to fall for it but she let Howard talk anyway.

"How about you stop talking down to the detective and pay attention to what she wants to ask?" Howard asked the man.

"Look, I'm all about cooperating with law enforcement but I have a stake in this part of the activities of the day and I need to be alert. Can't we do this in a mutually satisfactory way?"

"We will give you half an hour, but we aren't going anywhere. We'll be right here." Emilia leaned on the fence and watched a bit of the action.

It was slightly exciting but not something she was really interested in. She studied Myles Eisenger as he moved around in the arena. Those brothers sure were handsome and privileged but look where it got them. One in prison for murder and the other one a suspect in a second homicide.

She shocked herself with her next thought. What if Lincoln wasn't a bad guy? He *was* attractive. And she'd bet her service weapon that he wouldn't meow at his date. Or at least not on the first one. Shaking her head, she tried to clear the thoughts from her mind. It would do no good to develop a soft spot for either Eisenger brother.

Myles almost got pinned by the bull when the first rider fell but he deftly leapt aside. Maybe this sport was somewhat exciting after all. Emilia focused on the action.

When the rider got gored, she stepped back, appalled at the violence in the act. A little stunned that the warden and the state of Louisiana would allow this kind of thing to occur on the premises, she turned to the gray-haired man and, keeping the sarcasm to a minimum, asked, "What do you think? Time now for that cocoa?"

"I need to check on my bull."

"No, I think not. It's clear your bull is not harmed. He's the one who hurt the rider. It'll keep. We're going to ask our questions now." Howard held his arm out. "Do you want to go inside or do it right here?"

"Here is fine." The man leaned his hip on the fence. "Ask away."

Emilia pulled out her notebook and flipped toward the middle. "Do you drive a Volvo with a Louisiana plate of—" She read the numbers and letters off the page. "—GDH 12J?"

"Yeah, that's my car. Why?"

"You live in New Orleans?" she asked.

"I do. Again, why?"

"We're asking the questions here, sir." Howard held out his hand. "Let me see your driver's license, please."

The man pulled out his wallet and opened it to withdraw his license. He held it out.

Howard took the license and read to Emilia. "Michael Rhodes, lives at 682 Esplanade, age 64, height six feet. License expires in six months."

Emilia jotted down the information then addressed

Mr. Rhodes. "All right then, sir, now that we have your vitals, can you tell us what you were doing earlier this week, say Thursday, in the French Quarter, driving along and harassing young prostitutes?"

"*Excuse* me? What exactly are you trying to say here, lady?"

"I'm asking you what you were doing in the Quarter. Do you have an answer?"

"I do but I'm not going to talk to you anymore. It appears that you think I've committed some kind of crime. Don't think I haven't heard about those hookers who were killed and attacked. You and your partner here aren't going to pin that on me. If you have evidence to charge me with something, go ahead and do it. If you don't, you can make yourselves scarce. I don't have to talk to you. In fact, I'm going to call my lawyer right now." Rhodes pulled out a cell phone and scrolled down to a number.

"Come on, Em. I think we're done here." Howard glared at the man. "For now. Be assured that we will be in contact, Mr. Rhodes. You might want to tell that lawyer you seem to have on speed dial that we want a sit-down discussion with you tomorrow morning. Here's my card." Howard handed him a business card with the seal of the state of Louisiana embossed in gold on one corner. "Have him call first thing to arrange it."

Rhodes snatched the card from Howard's hand and pointedly turned his back on the two detectives.

As they strolled away, Emilia said, "I guess he showed us, didn't he?"

"Yeah, and interestingly, he didn't deny being involved. He merely said *if* you have evidence. I took that to mean that he thought we may, in fact, have some."

"Right. I took it to mean that there was no way we *did* have any and that, therefore, we couldn't haul him in if he chose not to cooperate."

"There in a nutshell, my dear partner, is the difference between us."

"What's that, Howard?"

"I see the half full glass and you see the half empty one."

"*Au contraire*, I see the *completely* empty one because I'm neither an optimist nor a pessimist. I'm a realist and the reality is, we have basically nothing on this guy or any other guy for that matter."

"When you're right, you're right." Howard followed her as she led the way back up to where the crowd was seated waiting for the calf roping to start.

Chapter 9

The roping events were interesting too but, after a few minutes, Linc excused himself to Patsy and her friends so he could go to the food vendors and get something to eat. He offered to bring them back something but they all turned him down. Once at the snack area, the smell of barbeque cooking made his stomach rumble.

He hadn't realized how hungry he was until he inhaled that wonderful aroma of smoking meat slathered in sauce.

He ordered a pulled pork sandwich, even though he really wanted to try the ribs, but they were too messy-looking to eat standing up. Once he had his sandwich in hand, he roamed around the vendors and admired the workmanship of the crafters as he ate.

"Look who's here," a voice behind Linc said.

He didn't want to turn around but knew he didn't

have a choice. It was his mother. Darn the luck. He'd been safer up there with Patsy and the ladies. He should've stayed put. He spun on his heel slowly. "Hello, Mother."

She held up her right cheek and he lightly kissed it as she expected.

She was very predictable. "I presume you're here to watch your brother make a fool of himself out there?"

"I'm here to be supportive of Myles, yes. What brings you and the politician here? It must be a good place to be seen by the voters because I'm sure you're not here to see your son."

"But look here." His mother spread her hands out. "I am seeing my son."

"That's ridiculous. You could see me any time in New Orleans. The fact that you ran in to me here is a complete accident. If you'd wanted to call and tell me you were coming up, we could have ridden together or arranged to meet and sit together. Since you didn't, I have to guess that you're here to somehow help that man you married in haste almost as soon as Daddy was in the grave."

"One of the major problems with you has always been your inability to rein in yourself. You say whatever comes into your head without thinking about the consequences of what you say."

Linc shook his head. "Are you kidding me?"

"Kidding how?"

"I think you must have me confused with someone else. I've never, ever had an issue like that. I don't even know what you're talking about."

"I'm talking about you and your rudeness to my husband. You're always saying unkind and downright rude things about him."

"That's not because I can't rein myself in. It's because I don't like the man. I don't plan to pretend that I do. Sorry. I can't betray my father's memory like that." Lincoln crumbled the paper his sandwich had been wrapped in.

"What about me? I'm still here and could use your support."

Before Linc could respond, the politician himself stepped up to stand beside his wife. The man was talking as he did so. "Got that all attended to down there. It's set. Let's go."

"What's set?" Linc asked the man whom he would never call stepfather.

"What are *you* doing here?" He turned to his wife. "Caroline, what's your son doing here?"

"In case you conveniently forgot, Senator Phelps, one of Caroline's sons is here full time." Linc smacked himself on the forehead. "Oh yeah. How *could* you forget? Myles's mother chose your campaign over helping her own son's criminal defense team. How quickly that slipped your mind."

"You're as rude as always, I see." The senator took

his wife by the elbow. "We're done here. Come on. I'm ready to go home."

"Ahh, yes, the home on St. Charles Avenue. My dad's house." Linc knew he was acting like a surly child but this man got under his skin worse than anyone in his life ever had.

"Lincoln Eisenger, there's no reason to be rude. Apologize to your stepfather right now."

Linc opened his mouth to respond but before he could, the announcer came on to say, "Time for the next most exciting part of the competition. The unbroken horse-riding event. As you fans know, every year, we bring in some fresh young horses who have never been ridden and some of our inmates agree to be the first rider on the backs of these magnificent creatures.

"As a special surprise today, we have a former national champion dressage competitor here to try to stay on one of these beauties. Mr. Myles Eisenger will be attempting his first ride on a wild horse right here in a few moments. Stay in your seats for that. It could be a fast event."

"What the hell?" Linc asked.

"Good question. What in the world is your brother thinking this time? He's always been rash and reckless."

"Again, Mother, you're totally wrong. Myles has always been steady and purposeful. I'm beginning to think you don't know either of your sons at all."

"Come, dear. Like I said, I'm ready to return to New

Orleans. There's no need to stay and watch this disaster play out." The senator seemed to be in a big hurry as far as Linc could tell.

"Don't you want to stay and watch?" Caroline asked.

"I certainly don't. Let's go." With those words, the senator and Mrs. Phelps turned away and left.

Linc didn't waste any time moving toward the area where he would be able to watch all the action coming up. He debated for a moment whether he should return to his seat or stand at the side where he was. Standing won out. He was nervous about the idea of Myles heading out there and risking his life on an unbroken horse. Was his brother really suicidal after all?

Within a few moments, a large black stallion was led into the chute area. He snorted and tossed his head to the left and then to the right. He stomped his feet and kicked up the dust. A few seconds later, the rider appeared. Gone were the goofy clown clothes and make up. This time Myles wore a regular cowboy hat, tight-fitting jeans, and a light denim long-sleeve shirt.

Myles settled himself on the horse's back while still in the stalls. The horse snorted and flung his head. His eyes rolled madly in their sockets. A sheen of sweet covered the animal as if he'd worked himself into some kind of frenzy.

Lincoln's stomach lurched. This did not bode well for his brother's safety and security.

It was too late for Linc to do anything to stop it. The

chute opened. Horse and rider bucked through the open-ing. For about five seconds it seemed as if Myles were going to make it and that Linc's fretting was for no rea-son but, in that sixth second, almost in slow motion, the rider lost his seat as even the horse lost its seat, too. The saddle fell to the ground on one side of the horse and the rider fell at the same time on the opposite side.

Linc was already running toward the entrance to the arena floor as his brother fell and landed with a thud on the hard dirt that formed the base for the facility. Myles lay very still on the ground. He didn't move.

⌘⌘⌘

Emilia ran toward the show area as soon as she saw the saddle slip off the side of the horse and on to the ground. Something didn't seem right about it. Yes, she got that it was hard for riders to stay on horses who'd never had a rider on them at all but this was over the top. This was the actual saddle falling off.

She called behind her, "Hurry, Howard. I think something bad is going down."

They raced to the side entrance of the dirt floor of the arena but were stopped by the guards from moving any farther. Emilia held out her special pass but one of the guards shook his head. "Sorry, ma'am, only prison offi-cials and emergency personal allowed."

Emilia stepped back but watched the action intently.

In a few seconds, the warden came by with an entourage. They all were moving quickly. A couple of paramedics with a gurney were right behind them and following in their wake was Lincoln Eisenger.

The same guard who stopped Emilia held his hand out to Linc. "You can't go past, sir."

"That's my brother. I want to see how he is."

"Sorry, man. I understand. I really do, but I can't let you past this barricade. You can stand right there and I can ask his condition for you." The guard turned to one of the others standing by. "Hey, John, go see if you can find out the status of the rider."

The announcer came over the speaker again. "Ladies and Gentlemen, please keep your seats until the emergency vehicles can get through to assist the rider. It looks like another delay but we'll get back to the action soon."

Emilia turned to Linc. "Sorry about your brother."

"Yeah, thanks. I appreciate the fact that, even though you think I'm a murderer, you have compassion for Myles. He doesn't deserve this."

"He's doing his time. I agree he doesn't need any accidents happening to make things harder." She nodded toward the ground where Myles still lay with the paramedics hovering over him. She decided not to respond to the murderer part of Linc's comment.

"Do you really think this was an accident?" Linc asked.

"You *don't?*" Emilia knew she had a suspicion that it

wasn't an accident but was it that obvious to a layman?

"No. I don't. I wanted to get over there where Myles is because I think that something's suspicious about that saddle. Saddles don't just fall off without help. Someone either put it on wrong or the straps were cut or the thing was somehow rigged to fail and thus harm my brother."

"How much do you know about horses, Mr. Eisenger?" Howard asked.

"Enough to know this stinks. Myles is a more than capable rider. While it's true that he's more of a European rider than a western rider, he has enough experience to put on a saddle correctly. I think someone else saddled that horse and had intent to harm him."

"But who would want to hurt your brother? He's in prison. What can he do to harm anyone?" Emilia asked. She truly didn't know what kind of motive someone would have to take action against Myles Eisenger.

"Like I've said at least a thousand times, the man was *falsely* convicted. We're working hard to free him. Maybe someone didn't want that to happen," Linc answered and then stepped over to have a whispered conversation with the guard who'd gone to check on his brother.

When the guard walked away and Linc turned to face the arena floor again, Emilia noticed how pale he had gone. She looked up at her partner and whispered, "Must be bad news. See how ashen Lincoln is?"

"Yeah. It doesn't look good. I don't think Myles has

moved a muscle since he fell. I wonder why the emergency techs don't get him to the ambulance and out of here. Surely it would be better to get him to the hospital sooner rather than later," Howard said.

As if his words were a signal to the EMTs, they seemed to have stabilized Myles enough to move him and, lifting the gurney up, started rolling it toward the exit.

When the gurney was next to where Lincoln stood, Emilia heard him say, "How bad is it and can I ride along? I'm his brother."

"You can follow us to the hospital. We won't have room for you. He has to be accompanied by a prison guard and, as it is, there's barely room for the guard since I'll need to be monitoring the patient closely."

Lincoln appeared unsteady on his feet. He swayed a bit as if buffeted by a high wind. "How bad is it?"

"He's probably concussed since he's still passed out and he may have internal bleeding. Look, we really need to get him out of here." The EMT nodded to his partner at the other end of the gurney and they moved out.

Lincoln followed close behind.

Emilia looked at Howard. "I want to get a look at that saddle."

"Not our case, Em. Fat chance of that happening."

"I'm going to try, anyway. My gut is screaming at me that this is somehow tied to our case."

"Which one? The hooker case or the murdered lawyer one?"

"The dead lawyer."

Howard rubbed his chin. "That would be odd, wouldn't it?"

"What would?"

"We came up here to question a witness or possible suspect to our hooker murder and, after getting the silent treatment from that witness, we find the man who we think may be involved in some way with the lawyer murder, based on the last words of the deceased that the receptionist told us. In addition to that, lo and behold, the brother of that suspect is injured in either a freak accident or an on-purpose attack and it all happens at the same venue. Makes you think, doesn't it?"

"Think what, Sherlock? Where's your brain headed on this?"

"I think we may actually only have *one* case."

"One case with multiple victims but all connected in some way?" Emilia nodded. "I'm convinced we need to mull that over and see if we can tie them together. I don't believe in coincidences."

"I don't either, partner. I don't either."

Chapter 10

Linc made it out to the parking lot in record time and, just as he got to his car, he heard the announcer state that the remainder of the rodeo had been canceled for the day. He opened his door and got in quickly so as not to get caught in the mass of people who would now be exiting the area. The ambulance driver had told him the name of the local hospital and Linc, with shaking fingers, put the name in his GPS and headed out the exit of the parking lot.

As he drove out, he idly wondered if his mother had heard that her son was injured and on the way to the hospital with a possible head injury and internal bleeding. He debated whether to call her and almost didn't but finally bit the bullet and made the call. She may have been a lousy mother in the past but she deserved a chance to be there for Myles if she wanted to.

He arrived at the hospital faster than he thought he

would and, after parking the car, he walked into the emergency room and identified himself as Myles's brother. The charge nurse said he was in the back already and undergoing some tests and she'd bring him a report soon. Linc got himself a cup of the free coffee available in the lobby and sat in one of the uncomfortable blue chairs.

The Weather Channel was on with its incessant chatter about various storms and weather patterns. Linc had long ago learned to turn out things like that and he sat in silence, periodically sipping on the thick sludge that passed as coffee in the place. He didn't know how much time had elapsed when his mother and her husband came in the sliding doors from the outside.

She sat beside him. "Thank you for calling. We were pretty far down the road to home and had to turn around. Is there any word on how he is?"

"Not yet." Linc shook his head. "Thanks for coming back. I told the nurse I was here but since you're technically next of kin, you might want to tell them that you've arrived. There may be some paperwork to sign since Myles wasn't able to sign for himself." Linc was a bit embarrassed to find that tears choked his throat and he was barely able to get out the last three words. This was his only brother. What if he died? How would he survive without Myles?

"I'll tell them when they update us." She glanced around the room and called out to her husband across the room. "Is there any coffee in that pot, dear?"

"Looks a bit nasty, darling. Do you want me to call someone to make a fresh pot?"

"No. I guess it's all right. I'll just wait."

"I saw a Starbucks down the road a little way. Want me to go get you a latte?" the senator asked.

"That would be lovely. Yes." She turned to Linc. "Would you like something?"

"No thanks."

Almost as soon as the man left the premises, the charge nurse came out and called, "Eisenger family?"

Linc and his mother stood. "Over here."

The nurse beckoned them over and they entered her small office area.

"They were able to wake the patient but he wasn't very alert. He has a subdural hematoma and is right now on the way to surgery for a spleen injury. He has some other internal injuries that will require some work while they're inside removing the spleen. The doctor asked if we could get each of you to provide some blood since the blood bank is low on Mr. Eisenger's type. Most of the time family members can donate and that helps. It's also pretty fast since we can do that right here and run the blood up to the surgical suite."

"I'll do it. Let's go." Linc stood and looked at his mother. "Are you in?"

She shook her head. "I don't think so."

"Why not? He's your son. Shouldn't you want to help?"

"I'm squeamish. I can't."

"That's a bunch of crap. I always knew you were a terrible excuse for a mother and this proves it. You've never cared one iota about Myles and me. Why are you even here?" Linc knew he was airing publically what he'd always wanted to keep under wraps—that his own mother hated her children—but he couldn't help it. All his worry about his brother was preying on his mind and affecting his judgment. But shouldn't the woman who gave birth to the boy want to do everything in her power to save him? What was a needle and some discomfort for a few moments compared to the life of her son?

"Lincoln. Sit." His mother's voice was calm and it made him even madder that she could perch there like some ice queen with her posture straight and not touching the back of the chair while his blood roiled in anger.

"No. I won't." He turned to the nurse. "Where do I go to give the blood?"

The woman stood. She clearly was uncomfortable with the direction of the conversation. "I'll take you to the back where the phlebotomist can draw the pint."

Linc laughed a grim bark of a laugh. "Sounds like a bartender. Drawing a pint." He followed the nurse out the door of her office and down a corridor to a set of double doors.

Before the doors opened, he heard the clack-clack of high-heeled pumps behind them. They both turned to find Linc's mother coming toward them. "I'll give blood. I'm not sure I'll be a suitable candidate but I'll try."

Maybe the woman was human after all. Linc smiled at her. "Thanks for trying."

"Like you said, it's the least I can do. He *is* my son, right?"

"Yes. He is."

The nurse hit a large metal button on the side of the wall and the double doors opened. She led them to a room with several recliners. She pointed to the chairs. "Sit and I'll have Mark come in and collect the blood in a few moments."

When she was gone, Caroline sat and glanced at Linc. "You sure know how to make someone feel like a real heel. I bet that talent comes in handy in the court-room."

"Yes, it does and, to be quite frank, I learned it from you."

"What does that mean?"

"It means that you were always on my case as a kid, as well as Myles's. What choice did we have but to learn from you? As you should well know, children watch their parents and emulate them. We got some of our worst characteristics from you."

"And I suppose all the good things about you were from your father?"

Linc realized what a jerk he was being. "Sorry. I didn't mean it that way. I'm worried about Myles and I'm afraid I'm taking it out on you."

"You always take everything out on me. I *did* try, you know. I tried to be a good mother to you two boys."

For a moment, Linc thought the woman was actually going to shed a tear but the moment passed when the phlebotomist entered the room. Once the man had drawn the blood, they each ate a cookie and drank some orange juice before they returned to the waiting room. The senator was there with the latte for his wife.

As soon as he saw her, he asked, "Where were you?"

"They wanted us to give blood for Myles. He's in surgery," Caroline said.

Senator Phelps visibly paled. "And you did? Was that a good idea, darling?"

Before she could answer, Linc asked, "What's the problem? Are you ill? Why shouldn't you be giving blood?" Now he really felt like a heel. Had he badgered a sick woman into doing something that could affect her own health? Geez. He needed to get a grip on his hostility for sure. What kind of man *was* he?

"No. I'm perfectly okay. He just knows how much I hate needles. It's fine, Linc. *I'm* fine."

Linc sat in the closest seat. "I'm glad to hear it."

"I bet you are. You've been on your mother's back since the minute she and I married. I bet you'd be glad if she were ill." The senator, who Linc refused to think of by his first name, Hugh, almost spat the words.

"I'd like to think that I'm not *that* much of a jerk, sir."

All Linc wanted to do was put his head in his hands and have some peace for a few moments but, as long as they were all stuck in this room together, that was not going to happen.

He glanced around the room. There were several more families in the area but they all seemed to be getting along. It gave him an idea. He stared at the senator. "Sir, I think some of the people here may be voters. You might want to rein in your animosity toward me and pretend that you're on the campaign trail. Maybe kiss a baby or two."

Hugh Phelps seemed to take in his surroundings at that comment and Linc was amazed to see the transformation in him. He'd never witnessed the change from moody stepfather mode to politician mode. It was truly something to behold.

The man spent the next moments, as his wife sipped her latte, doing the glad-hand, I'm-so-proud-to-meet-you act that seemed to charm voters and non-voters alike. He did actually kiss one of the babies in the room who proceeded to wail and fuss.

Before the senator made the full rounds of the room, the charge nurse came out again and called for the Eisenger family. The lack of a smile or any other emotion on her face made Linc's heart sink. This didn't look good.

退役

Howard and Emilia stood in the warden's office, talking to him and the local detectives who'd been called in on the case. The belly strap on the saddle that Myles Eisenger was on had been sliced in such a way that it could only have been sabotage. It had started out holding together but was cut on each end enough to cause a fray. As the horse bucked, the strap would have rubbed against the animal and torn the rest of the way through.

The local cops had questioned the man who placed the saddle on the horse but he swore it was fine and intact at the time he left the paddock area. They were now making the rounds, questioning everyone who had been anywhere near the action of the rodeo. The warden was understandably upset and on edge because of the two injuries. The goring one was clearly an accident but since there would be an investigation into the injury to Myles Eisenger, the warden wanted both incidents to be included.

Emilia and Howard were allowed in the meeting since they'd indicated to the assistant warden that they thought their murders were tied up in the attack on Myles. The assistant, in turn, spoke to the warden about letting them in on the investigation. Grateful to be included, they both kept quiet throughout the meeting until the warden addressed them.

"Detective Mills, can you add anything to what we've discussed?"

"Not really other than to say that we plan to get the

evidence files from Mr. Eisenger's murder case to see if we can find anything that may have been missed. It seems to us that this purposeful injury to him leads back in some way to either his conviction or his law firm. I think it's worth looking at."

"I agree. The fact that you have a murdered lawyer from Eisenger's office and today an attempt is made on my inmate has to be connected somehow. It's beyond credulity that they wouldn't be related," the warden said.

"We'll keep you updated as well as the local guys. I hope we'll get the same courtesy from you." Howard turned to Emilia. "I think we want to drop by the hospital before we return to New Orleans. We want to check on Eisenger's condition."

"I'm going to send a guard over for the night to relieve the one who rode over in the ambulance. I'll let him know you'll be in the area. Maybe if the boy wakes up soon, we can all have a little chat and see if he remembers anything. He may have seen someone around the horses and saddles or something else odd." The warden glanced over at the local chief of police. "This is some mess we got here. Can we all coordinate our efforts to see if we can find the culprit or culprits?"

The man nodded. "We sure can. Starting with a joint interview with Eisenger once he's awake and alert enough to talk."

"Are we sure that brother of his will let him talk? He's pretty set that Myles was wrongfully convicted. He may not want him talking to law enforcement at all," Emilia said.

"I think Lincoln Eisenger will want to get to the truth as much as we do. I've seen him here visiting his brother and have had conversations with him over the years. He's a reasonable man. He used to practice criminal work in his early days as a lawyer before he joined his family's firm. He was planning to be a reformer but the system got to him and he moved over to the more lucrative side. He's a smart man. He won't stand in our way," the warden said.

"I hope you're right." Emilia shoved herself off the wall where she'd been leaning during the meeting. "I'm ready to get to work."

"We'll send you the first witness interviews in the morning." The local police chief shook Howard and Emilia's hands. "When you get through that evidence box, let us know what you uncover."

"We will." Howard saluted the warden. "We'll meet your guy at the hospital."

Emilia and Howard left the prison, turning in their temporary ids as they passed the checkpoint. The crowd in the parking lot had thinned considerably while they were inside and, before they knew it, they were at the lobby doors to the emergency room.

"What's the best approach to Eisenger? We know he thinks we're the Anti-Christ out to get him and his brother."

"Em, I think that we tell the man the truth."

She crossed her arms over her stomach. "What truth?"

"That we need his help. That we plan to look into his brother's situation—both at the prison and his conviction—that we think they may be related to each other as well as to Van Nuys' death."

"What about the prostitutes?"

"I say we leave that out for now. Need to know basis is all we should give him right now."

"Okay. Good cop, bad cop?" Emilia grinned.

"No. How about honest, pleading cop?"

Emilia laughed. "You *do* know that's way harder for me, right?"

"Yes, I do but you'll have to suck it up and manage it." Howard stepped on the mat that cued the doors to open. As he stepped into the lobby, he said, "Show time."

Emilia was right behind him. She stopped short as she recognized Senator Phelps seated beside a blonde woman elegantly coiffed in what some would refer to as a helmet-style haircut. The type that was sprayed so much that it didn't move in the wind or when the person shook her head. The woman was beautiful even in her late forties or early fifties and, after a moment, Emilia recognized her as the senator's wife. Wasn't there some kind of scandal about the haste of their marriage? Emilia shrugged. It didn't matter to her. She did idly wonder what they were doing here in the emergency room.

Lincoln gazed across the space as if he were curious who had entered. When his eyes landed on Emilia, his face turned red and she swore that steam came out of his ears. He leapt to his feet and covered the distance from his chair to her in four large strides. "What the hell are you doing here? My brother's in recovery and we're all worried about him. We don't have the time or the inclination for your nonsense."

Emilia couldn't help herself. She knew she'd promised Howard to be nice and that she would do her level best to convince Lincoln Eisenger to work with them but she had to ask. "*We*? Who's we?"

"My mother over there with her husband and me." He pointed to the senator and his wife.

That was his mother? What kind of detective was she not to know that?

Howard stepped forward between Linc and Emilia. He nudged her with his foot and she stepped aside. She really had to learn to hold back when it came to this man, Lincoln.

"I'm sorry your brother was hurt, Mr. Eisenger." Howard held his hand out. "We're actually here to try to get your assistance."

"*My* assistance? I'm sorry. I fail to understand how, or more importantly, *why*, I'd want to help the NOPD after all they've done to my family and are trying to do to me?"

"May we sit down and discuss it?" Howard indicated

a bank of chairs over near the corner of the room.

"Since I have nowhere else to be until I can see my brother, I'll listen to what you want to say but let me tell you right off the bat, if that woman there—" He nodded at Emilia. "—starts her crap with me again, it's all over and I'll be asking you to leave."

"Fine. It's a deal." Howard glanced at Emilia. She nodded and then he added, "See? She's in."

"Right. We'll see." Lincoln led the way to the corner.

When they were seated, Emilia bit the bullet and apologized. "I'm sorry. I didn't recall that your mother was married to Senator Phelps. I shouldn't have been so rude."

Linc nodded at her. "Wow. If I wasn't so suspicious about what you and your partner want from me, I might even believe that you were sincere in that apology."

"I really am sorry. It wasn't the best way to start our conversation."

"Whatever. It doesn't matter. What did you need, Detective Mills?" Linc faced Howard and directed his question at him.

"We think the attack on your brother today is somehow related to the death of your law partner and—"

"Let me guess. You think I did this, too?" Linc's face turned red again. "I'd never hurt my brother. He's the only family I have."

"Wait a second. You just said your mother is over

there." Emilia tilted her head toward the woman and the senator.

"I did. She *is* my mother but she's more family with the senator than my brother and me. Without going into details about my personal life, suffice it to say that *Myles* is my family."

As Emilia watched, Lincoln seemed to realize what she and Howard were doing and the lawyer did a double take. "Wait. You think what happened to Myles wasn't an accident?"

"Don't you?" Emilia asked.

"Well, yeah, I confess that the thought did pass through my mind but no one seemed to be that concerned about it out at the rodeo grounds." Linc ran his hands through his hair. "You mean you're investigating it?"

"Not exactly. We're out of our jurisdiction up here but the local folks and the warden agree that this was no accident. We're going to look at Myles's case and see if there's something in the murder trial files that was missed. Maybe a reason that someone wants him out of the way," Howard said.

"And you want me to do what?"

"Share your notes with us. We know you've been trying to prove your brother was wrongfully convicted and have an investigator working on it with you. We'd like to see his notes as well." Howard tapped his own forehead. "You know, put our heads together, so to speak."

"But I'm still a suspect in the death of Van Nuys?"

"You haven't been cleared, as of now, so I have to say yes to that question," Howard said.

Lincoln sat back for several minutes with the thumb of his right hand rubbing his chin. Finally, he said, "I have a proposition for you."

"What's that?" Emilia asked with a sense of dread.

What kind of bargain with the devil were they going to have to make in order to solve her first real case since becoming a detective? Her heart heavy, she braced herself to hear what Lincoln was going to say.

"I want to know first what you think you have on me. Why am I on the short list of suspects?" Linc's lips made a thin smile. "Is that a deal breaker, Detective Hammond? Can you bear to share with me like you want me to share with you?"

Chapter 11

The door that led to the treatment rooms opened. A woman in scrubs came forward and called for the Eisenger family.

Linc excused himself from the detectives. He and his mother walked over to speak to the woman. He was glad to see that the senator kept back and let them get the news—whatever it was—by themselves.

"Myles came through the surgery well. He's out of recovery but still a little groggy. I'm going to let you both in for a few moments to see him. We brought him down from the surgical ward because the warden wanted him to remain under guard since he's an inmate. We have a secure facility on this floor because we service the prison. I'm going to let you see him for about fifteen minutes, but that's it."

"Aren't there some policemen who need to question

him about what happened out there at the arena?" Linc asked.

"That will have to wait. He's in no condition to answer questions since he's still on the morphine drip. I'm only letting you back so you can see that he's all right. Then he is going to be left alone to sleep off all the sedation and recover some. The cops will be waiting until morning."

The nurse's tone was no nonsense. It made Linc comfortable that she would guard his brother better than the state prison employees would.

"Let's see him then." Lincoln glanced at his mother. "Ready?"

"Yes. I can only stay a few moments. Hugh needs to get back to New Orleans. We're already late."

Determined not to let the woman under his skin, Linc ignored her comment and followed the nurse down another corridor to a steel door with an armed guard outside. She keyed in a code and when a click sounded, she pushed the door open.

Before he entered, Linc touched the nurse lightly on the arm. "What happens if there's an emergency and someone has to get in fast? I'm concerned about that keypad."

"It can be bypassed if necessary. There shouldn't be any problem with your brother. He's had his spleen removed, has a couple of broken ribs, a broken arm, and a concussion. We don't anticipate any irregularities that would cause a code red like a heart attack or anything like that. Be assured, we'll take good care of Myles."

"All right, I'm going to trust you on this," Linc said.

"I'm going to leave you alone to chat with your brother but I'll be right outside if you need me."

"Thank you." Linc stepped aside to allow Caroline to enter first. "Mother, you go ahead."

She passed by him and he got a whiff of her too strong perfume. She stepped over to the end of the bed and eyed her son who was staring at her, too. "How are you feeling?" she asked.

"I'm pretty banged up but it looks like I'll survive."

Linc moved inside as well but he went to the head of the bed where he could get a good look at his brother. Glad that he was able to talk and *did* seem all right, Linc took a deep shuddering breath before he trusted himself to say anything.

When he had his wits about him, he tapped Myles on the cast on his right arm. "Hell of a thing out there, little brother."

"You're telling me."

"I'm sorry this happened to you, Myles. Hugh and I have been waiting outside for hours and now that I've seen that you're going to be fine, I really need to be going. He's missed a meeting this evening and needs to get back to the city. I'm sure you understand." Caroline patted the end of the bed.

"Sure, Mother. I understand. I'm sorry to have inconvenienced you and the senator. Next time, I'll try to do better," Myles said.

"It's all right, dear. He'll manage to get the meeting rescheduled. I'll call to check on you tomorrow." She turned and walked out of the room.

As soon as she was gone, Lincoln snickered. "Does she even know what she says?"

"I don't think so. She's clueless."

"Selfish is more like it."

"Linc, I need to say something before that nurse comes back."

"You think someone sabotaged your saddle?"

"Yes. I do. How'd you know?"

"It seems the police think so, too. They're out in the lobby now but they aren't going to be able to talk to you until tomorrow since the doctor says you need to rest for now. Let me ask you, though, did you see who did it?"

"No." Myles shook his head. "I didn't see anyone but almost as soon as the gate from the chute rose and that horse took off, I knew I was in trouble. The saddle seemed wrong from the start. There was nothing I could do. I was sure I was going down."

"I'm glad you made it. I have to tell you, it was very scary seeing you lying there on the ground and not moving. Scared the crap out of me. You know it's you and me against the world, right? If something happened to you, it'd be only me."

"We need to find you a bride then because, even

though I'm going to survive, sadly, I'll be back in prison the moment I'm discharged from this place."

"I'm still working on that."

"What? A bride? What are you keeping from me?"

Myles winked and Linc knew he was trying to put on a brave face because of the fact that he was still an inmate of the state's maximum security prison.

"No. There's no bride on the horizon. I'll be sure to let you know if that happens."

The door opened and the nurse in scrubs reappeared. "Time to let the patient get some rest. We're going to bring a light dinner tray and then maybe we'll let you watch a little television before you go to sleep."

"Well, there's a bright spot anyway, bro." Myles said to Linc.

"What's that?"

"I'm not in the community room and I'll get to pick a television show I want to watch instead of one that the bigger guys want to see."

"Have you been mistreated by the other inmates?" Linc didn't like hearing that Myles had fears of the bigger men in the prison. He knew it was a fact of prison life that some inmates bullied others but it caused him even more concern about his brother.

"Nah. Don't you worry about that. I steer clear of them. I usually play cards or read instead of trying to watch the TV."

Myles smiled but Linc could see the lie in his eyes.

His brother truly was afraid of some of the other inmates.

The nurse took hold of Linc's arm. "Time to go. You can come back tomorrow to see him. He'll be here a few days before he's transported back to the prison where he'll be in the infirmary."

Linc nodded over the lump in this throat. He was more determined than ever to see his brother freed from his own personal hell. And if it meant working with the NOPD to make it happen, so be it.

♋♋♋

While Lincoln was in the other part of the hospital with Myles, Emilia paced in tight circles in the space in front of the chair where Howard sat. This idea of cooperation with Eisenger sounded great in theory but when it came right down to it, actually to tell him what they had to tie him to Van Nuys' death seemed a bit immature to her. If they disclosed it, chances were Linc would be able to think of a reason why the man said what he said as he was dying.

She didn't want to give away their advantage with no guarantee that it would be worth the tradeoff.

"Will you stop walking around like that and sit down? Tell me what has you all spun up."

"I think it's a mistake to give Eisenger the information he wants. Shouldn't we wait and see what the police evidence box holds and read the transcript of the trial before we make a tradeoff with him? Maybe we don't need his investigator or his notes."

"I think it's worth the risk."

Emilia flopped herself into the chair beside Howard. "I'm not so sure. I wish I was."

"It's a risk we have to take. Remember, you're trying to prove yourself, not only to your family on this case, but to the entire city of New Orleans. You have no choice if you want to solve this case spectacularly."

"Stop teasing me. It's a serious thing. I want to more than prove myself and it's not something to joke about. It's quite, quite serious."

"Then suck it up and talk to the man." Howard glanced up. "Look, here comes Linc's mother. He'll probably be right behind her. Time to decide if you're in or out."

"I'm in. You know I am." Emilia watched the senator's wife as she interacted with her husband.

They seemed perfect for each other. The woman appeared to hang on every word the man said and the man acted as if she were the only person in the room. Emilia wasn't sure how much she liked the woman, because she was a bit of a snob, but Caroline was definitely a lucky woman when it came to the man she loved. He obviously loved her like no other. It was all over his face that he practically worshipped the lady. Emilia was a little envious of that. She knew she would probably never be the recipient of such a great love.

She wondered what kind of marriage the woman had been in when she was married to Lincoln's father. Could that woman have been lucky enough to have not one but two men love her to the extent her current husband did? Talk about having more than your share of good things happening to you.

"Are you still there?" Howard asked.

"What do you mean?"

"You were miles away. What were you thinking?"

"I was wondering about Linc and his mother. It seemed a bit off to me that when we came in, she and her husband were on the opposite side of the room from Lincoln. It's weird. Most families would pull together when someone was hurt or in surgery. They were acting like two sides in a boxing match. Each in their own corner and only talking to each other when the rules required it. Doesn't it seem odd to you?"

"Yeah but it's none of our business."

"You're right but it's still curious."

The senator and his wife left the building. In a few moments, Lincoln came strolling in.

He headed straight toward the two detectives. "Can we go to the local Waffle House and get something to eat before returning to New Orleans? I'm starved and I want to hear what you have to say about the Van Nuys case."

"Sure. I could use a meal, too." Howard stood and smiled at Emilia. "You hungry?"

"You bet. Let's go."

When they got to the parking lot, Linc checked his phone for the nearest Waffle House and they agreed on the one they would meet at which was located a few miles down the road.

They each drove at their own pace and Linc arrived before the detectives. He went in and got a table. As he watched them pull in, he paid attention to their body language since he'd taken a seminar in that subject and liked to use what he learned in order to try to gain an advantage in the courtroom. He'd decided he could use that also to pick up clues about his new cohorts, whom he still distrusted even though he'd agreed to work with them.

He watched them walk toward the restaurant. They were obviously comfortable with each other. They laughed and seemed at ease. There didn't seem to be anything sexual between them, just a great friendship and respect. He certainly thought that Mills was a calmer, more rational cop than his female partner but they did make a good team with their varying personalities.

They came in and made their way to the booth in the corner that Lincoln had taken. They sat opposite him and glanced down at the menus Linc had already gotten from the waitress.

After they ordered, Linc said, "What's the deal then?"

"What deal?" Emilia asked.

Linc stared at her for a full minute. Finally, he shook his head. "Can I say something?"

She shrugged.

"Look, I get that you don't like me. I *do* understand that but we've got to put our differences behind us if we're going to have any chance at all of getting this mess resolved. Do you agree?"

"I do and I promise to try harder but it seems to me that everything you say sets my teeth on edge. I can't help it. That's how I react."

"You definitely have to work harder at controlling those reactions, then. Maybe I can help you."

"How's that?"

She couldn't help but smile. He seemed to be working some charm offensive on her. His voice was soothing and calm and she got a sense of well-being that flooded over her. How was he doing that?

"A technique I learned in law school to help me cope with obnoxious professors and that I've used since then with reluctant or belligerent witnesses on the stand."

"What's that technique?"

"I first count to ten backward, which is standard advice, but then I take it farther and, lowering my voice a couple of octaves, I speak in a low tone and with a small lilt. Seems to work to settle people down."

"Looks like it worked on her, Eisenger," Howard said. "She's actually smiling at you. Can you believe that?"

Linc laughed. "I confess, I never thought it would happen. At least not in this lifetime."

"If you two are done making fun of me, can we get to it? We came here to compare notes, not to use technique on the girl detective."

Linc laughed again. "Using technique sounds a little pornographic, Detective Hammond."

"Never mind." A bit embarrassed, Emilia ducked her head down. Yep, she could see how he got those big dollar verdicts in his cases. He could slather on the charm pretty thickly when he needed to.

"You two have had enough time to discuss whether or not you're willing to tell me what you have that makes me a suspect in Van Nuys's death so what's it going to be? To tell or not to tell?"

"Here's the thing, Eisenger," Howard said. "The victim said a couple of words to the receptionist as he was dying."

"What did he say?"

"He said, Linc, Linc."

Howard stared at Lincoln as did Emilia. She knew they were both gauging his reaction.

"You think he said my name? Do you think he was saying that I was his killer?"

"Seems logical, doesn't it?" Emilia asked.

"I can see how you might think so, but how do you know he was saying my name? Couldn't he actually be saying something about a link—you know, as in a link to something else? As in L-I-N-K not my nickname of L-I-N-C?"

The two detectives looked at each other. Emilia wondered if Howard was thinking the same thing she was, that Van Nuys's death was *linked* to the prostitute's murder. Dear God, how had they been so blind? Why did they both leap to the same conclusion that the dead man was trying to name his killer?

"I can see that this is the first you two have considered this possibility," Linc said as the waitress placed their orders on the table. "I can also see how you might make the jump to connect me to the death, since you had an Eisenger already convicted of murder and another one in the same firm as Van Nuys. But I sure wish you had taken a moment to consider that he may have meant something else before focusing your sights on me."

"We still don't know it wasn't your name he was saying but we *will* try to look at it from this other angle now." Emilia smiled to take the edge off what she was going to say next. "But be assured if the evidence points to you, we're still going to go down that path."

Linc nodded and speared some of his scrambled egg. "Fair enough." He took a bite and chewed.

Howard and Emilia dug into their breakfast for dinner as well.

In a moment, Linc looked up at them. "Seems to me that this spirit of cooperation may bring benefits to us all."

"I hope so, Mr. Eisenger," Howard said.

"You might as well call me Linc if we're going to be partners."

"Better not. What if all roads lead to you?" Emilia asked.

"I can assure you that they won't, but let's agree that if you find yourself in the situation where you have to arrest me, you can call me Mr. Eisenger again but, until then, I prefer Linc. Is that acceptable?" He placed his fork on his plate and held his hand out to shake hers.

After staring at his for a moment, she stretched out her own. "Fair enough." She paused a beat before taking his hand. "Linc."

His handshake was gentle and his skin warm and dry. He smiled. "See, that didn't hurt at all. You didn't even stutter over it."

Howard cracked up and, after giving him a dirty look, Emilia found herself laughing as well. It was a few moments before she realized that Linc still held her hand. She pulled it away and tried to focus on her plate but she was acutely aware of the man across the table.

Chapter 12

After a night of tossing and turning, Emilia woke early, thinking that she'd only slept about fifteen minutes all night. She groaned and turned over onto her stomach. They'd gotten back from Angola pretty late the evening before and she was sure it was going to shape up to be yet another long day. Massive quantities of caffeine would be needed.

She tossed the covers off her legs and staggered to the one-wall kitchen area of her efficiency apartment. Grateful that she'd had the forethought to get the coffee ready to brew before she went to bed, she pushed the button to turn on the machine. The sound of the liquid sizzling into the carafe and the aroma of the beans helped to wake her a little. She opened the package of bread on the counter, put a slice in each side of the toaster, and pressed down on the handle.

While her breakfast was cooking, she ran her hands

through her hair and thought about a plan of action for the day. They were to meet with Linc at ten a.m. and go over some of his notes. Emilia expected she and Howard would get the evidence files on Myles's case from archives when they got in around eight. She knew at some point in the day that she would have to become Amy the hooker and see if she could find some of the other girls to chat up about the attacks on them. Lord, she dreaded getting into that get-up. She poured herself some coffee.

When her toast popped up, Emilia grabbed a paper towel and placed them on it. She headed to the bathroom to get ready, munching on one of the pieces. She turned the water on in the shower and waited for it to get hot. While waiting, she ate the other slice of dry toast. She wished she had some beignets but Alyce-Faye didn't ride to the rescue today.

On her way out the door, Emilia's cell phone rang. She accepted the call and spoke into the mouthpiece. "Hammond."

"Em, it's Howard. I'm going to be late today. Momma had some kind of scare with her heart last night and I'm at the hospital with her. They're still doing some tests."

"Is she going to be okay?"

"We think so. Should know something later this afternoon. I was calling to see if you think you can handle getting the evidence and meeting with Linc without me."

"Of course I can. Piece of cake."

"I'll be there as soon as I can. Be nice, okay?"

"I'm always nice. Call me as soon as you know something about you mother." Emilia clicked off the call and left her apartment to head to the evidence archives.

When she had what she needed, she drove to the precinct and parked. She carried the box to Linc's office. It was conveniently near the precinct so she opted to walk as opposed to trying to park at his building since there was always a lot of traffic in that area.

Inside the office building, she signed in. The same rent-a-cop was on duty as when they'd entered the building to interview Linc the day Van Nuys died. Emilia didn't try to make conversation with him but she did recall the lady in the green dress who had run past her and Howard that day.

She needed to make a note to try to find out who that person was. Maybe the woman had seen something and that was why she was so rattled when she collided with Emilia.

Hiking the box onto her hip, Emilia pushed the elevator button. On the fourth floor, the door opened to the lobby that she recognized from the other evening. Someone had come in and cleaned the floor. Talk about efficiency. The tan carpet looked brand new.

Emilia stepped over to the receptionist's desk. The lady called Maggie was not the woman seated there. Emilia wondered if she'd quit after the murder. "I'm detective Hammond here to see Lincoln Eisenger."

"I think he may be at the courthouse. Let me buzz his assistant."

"Sure." That would be just like the man to tell her to come to his office to go over the evidence and then not be here himself. Emilia barely refrained from tapping her toe.

In a few seconds, the woman Emilia recognized from the other evening came around the corner. She stopped in front of Emilia. "Good morning, Detective. I don't know if you recall, but I'm Greta Greensboro. Mr. Eisenger got called in on an emergency hearing with Judge Nicholson. He told me to let you and your partner—" Greta glanced around as if looking for the missing Howard. "—into the conference room so you can get started. He'll be back as soon as he can. Where is your partner?"

"He had an emergency himself so it looks like it's going to be me alone. I could head back to the precinct and return later."

"Nonsense. Come into the conference room. There are some legal pads and pens already in there. You can get going here and I'll bring you some coffee. How's that?"

Since the box seemed to be getting heavier by the second and another dose of caffeine sounded great, Emilia nodded. "All right. I don't want to impose but—"

"It's not an imposition. Linc already had the conference room reserved so you might as well use it. Do you recall where it is?"

"Yeah. I can find my way. It's down this hall, right?" Emilia tilted her head in the direction she remembered they'd taken the witnesses to wait for their interviews when Van Nuys died.

"It is. I'll be in with the coffee in a few moments."

Emilia made it to the conference room and pushed the door open with her hip before staggering across the carpet to flop the box onto the table. She stretched her arms to bring the feeling back into them. They were numb and achy from carrying the box for so long.

Eventually, when she trusted her arms to work again, Emilia lifted the lid off the box and started to sort through the individual evidence bags. She pulled a legal pad toward her and began an inventory list of her own to compare to the one on the top of the box. One of the things she'd learned over the years was that sometimes evidence got lost, misplaced, or misfiled. She wanted to be sure it was all here and accounted for.

When she was about half through the contents of the box, Greta came in with the coffee. "I wasn't sure how you took it so I brought it on a tray with some sweetener and creamer."

"Thanks. I take it black."

"I figured you might since I'd heard you're a native but you never know."

"Where did you hear that?"

Greta shrugged. "I don't know. Someone must have told me that."

"I *am* from Algiers, but I didn't know it was common knowledge."

Always suspicious, Emilia wondered why this woman would've been asking questions about her. People didn't just talk about where cops were from in idle conversation. Emilia remembered Howard telling her to be nice so she elected not to push the woman on why she knew where she was from.

"I think it's more common knowledge that you're from the Hammond family of New Orleans law enforcement," Greta said. "There's that African-American captain Emil Hammond who was all over the news after Hurricane Katrina when he helped a lot of people in the ninth ward. Aren't you related to him? Your name is pretty close, isn't it? Emil and Emilia? Don't you have family all over the NOPD?"

"I don't know that I'd go so far as to say they are all over the NOPD but yes, I have a grandfather, father, two brothers, and a couple of cousins on the force."

This was getting weirder and weirder. This lady really had checked up on her. Did Linc instruct her to do so when they'd been assigned to investigate him? Did the Greta woman have information on Howard as well?

"Enjoy the coffee. I'll check in on you later." Greta turned to leave the room.

The door opened to Lincoln Eisenger. He wore what even Emilia could tell was a very expensive navy blue suit. He had on a white shirt with a navy blue stripe and a navy and gray tie with a slanted stripe pattern. He was breathtakingly handsome. Emilia found herself staring and ducked her head down to cover her embarrassment.

"Sorry I'm late. Judge Nicholson set a hearing on a discovery dispute for this morning." Linc glanced around the room. "Where's Howard?"

"He had somewhere to be first thing as well. He'll join us soon." Emilia made eye contact with Linc as soon as she sensed that she could without letting him know he'd rattled her.

"Greta, I could use some coffee, too. Can you grab me some while Emilia and I get to work?" Linc shucked off his jacket, tossed it on the back of one of the maroon leather chairs, and loosened his tie. When Greta nodded and left the room, Linc grinned at Emilia. "Alone at last." He sat opposite her.

She gaped at him. What did that mean? Was he serious or was that more of the charm she'd learned he could turn on and off at will? Was he trying to catch her off-guard? He'd already disturbed her equilibrium when he stepped into the conference room, all sexy and scruffy, with that partial beard that had always been her undoing when it came to men.

∽∾∽

Linc wanted to laugh. He'd been trying to get Detective Hammond to behave like a normal woman since almost the moment he'd met her. She was a tough nut to crack. She had a hard outer shell but he could sense vulnerability under the façade. He wanted to probe around her psyche and uncover what was really there. He had no clue what he'd done or what Greta had said before he came into the conference room but something had disturbed Emilia. She had blushed a lovely shade of pink before she hid her face. The freckles across her nose were more prominent when her cheeks colored.

For a brief second, those freckles jarred some memory almost to the surface but he couldn't quite capture it. What could it be? It niggled at his mind but he needed to focus on the evidence box now. While he had watched his brother's trial with great interest from the gallery, this was his first opportunity to touch and handle the exhibits and documents.

"Have you made any progress?" Linc asked Emilia.

"I've been inventorying the box. I like to check first to be sure it's all here."

"What's the verdict? Anything missing?"

"I can't seem to find exhibit twenty-three. That's the only thing not here."

"What is number twenty-three?" Linc moved to the same side of the table as Emilia and sat beside her.

She pushed her handwritten list toward him then grabbed the official list of exhibits. She pointed to the number. "See here? It says *property deeds/trust*. What is that?"

"I'm not sure. We have a family trust that holds interest in some real estate, including this building but I don't remember it coming up in Myles's trial. I need to go get the transcript. Hang on a minute." He rose from his seat and went to his office. On the way, he passed Greta with his coffee.

"Did you need something, Mr. Eisenger?"

"Going to get the transcript of my brother's trial. You can leave the coffee in the conference room. Thanks."

"I don't think the transcript is in your office."

Linc came to a dead stop. "Where else would it be?"

"I think that investigator guy you hired came by and picked it up the other day."

"You *think*? You think? Why don't you know?" Linc reined in his temper but barely. She knew that his brother's case was the main focus of his attention. Why would she let that transcript go out of the office and not know where it was?

"Okay, okay, sorry. The investigator has it. He said he wanted to read it to see if there was anything he could follow up on as a lead." Her hand shook and some of the coffee spilled over the edge of the cup and on to the carpet.

"Get it back. Today." Linc spun on his heel and returned to the conference room with Greta on his heels. He jerked the door open and retook his place beside Emilia.

Greta came in and set the coffee cup on the table.

"I'll make that call, Mr. Eisenger." She left the room.

"Where's the transcript? I thought you went to get it," Emilia asked.

"That's the call Greta is making. It seems she loaned out the transcript without my permission. My only copy."

"What about your notes from the work you've been doing? Your investigator's notes?"

"They're all at my house, thank God." Linc shook his head in disbelief of Greta's actions. "I can't, for the life of me, figure out why she let that document leave the building. She's never been so irresponsible before."

"Maybe she thought she was helping? Who'd she give it to?"

"It was my investigator but she could have made him a copy instead of giving him the only one we had."

"At least she gave it to a friend and not a foe and she can get it back. Let's move forward and look at what we have now. We can figure out that missing exhibit later." Emilia opened one of the plastic bags. "We can look inside these but when we close them, I have to initial and date the bag so let's only open one at a time, okay?"

"Okay by me." Linc watched her slide a firearm out of the bag. "That's the murder weapon?"

"Yeah. Did Myles own a gun? Look at the serial number here—actually, look at the lack of serial number—see how it's been shaved off? How did they tie it to your brother?" Emilia ran her index finger over a scratched place on the side of the weapon.

"His prints were on it. He said it was because he was stupid and picked it up in a panic when he found the victim."

"That's kind of hard to believe. I mean, no offense but he's a lawyer. Wouldn't he know better than to touch a firearm that may have been used at a shooting? One that was right beside a dead person?"

"The prosecution emphasized that over and over with the jury. They also came up with some crazy story that Myles bought the gun from some guy in Pirates Alley. I've got my investigator trying to find that witness who said he saw the transaction but so far, nothing. It's like the man disappeared off the planet."

"That's interesting." Emilia rubbed her chin. "Yeah. Very interesting."

"What?" Did she have an inspiration? Was she going to come out with some great clue or lead?

"Sounds like either a jail house snitch or a bribed witness to me. Have you checked the local lockup or the county jails?"

"We were focusing on the Pirates Alley area not the jails."

"Usually someone willing to lie in court—if it *was* a lie, mind you—is someone who already has a record and no respect for the system. Do you remember the witness's name? Maybe it's someone Howard or I have heard of before."

"Yeah. I remember his name. I'll never forget it. I just wish we could find him."

"What's the name?"

"Simon Bolger."

Emilia gasped and put her hands up to her cheeks.

"*What*? You know this guy?"

"I do indeed, Lincoln Eisenger, and I have to say, if Simon Bolger had his hand in your brother's conviction, dear God in heaven, your brother *is* innocent and has truly been railroaded."

She leapt out of her chair so fast it fell to the carpet with a loud thud that shook the floor. She paced the area between the conference room table and the window until Linc came out of his own seat and caught her by the upper arms.

"What? What? What do you know about this man?" Linc practically yelled the words.

He couldn't decide if he was ecstatic that finally someone in law enforcement believed him about Myles or if he was filled with dread as the man he'd named was clearly bad, bad news.

Chapter 13

Someone flung the door back on its hinges. It smacked the wall on the other side. Emilia's head whipped around at the sound. Greta stood in the opening and asked, "Is everything all right? Mr. Eisenger, do I need to call security?"

"No. Why would you do that?" Linc asked.

Greta nodded at Linc's hands where they were clutching Emilia's biceps. "You appear to be restraining the detective and we all heard raised voices from in here."

He dropped his hands. "Uh, sorry. We found something interesting and got a little loud. Everything is fine. Go on back to work."

Greta took a step inside the room. "What did you discover?"

"Never mind," Emilia responded before Linc could say anything. "We're keeping it to ourselves."

Greta turned her gaze to Linc. "Is that true?" Her eyes filled with tears. "You want to keep it a secret? Maybe I can help."

"If the detective says not to share, I don't share. Sorry, Greta."

"Since when did you start listening to cops?"

"Since he asked me and my partner for help."

Emilia didn't like the snooty legal assistant who seemed to think Linc Eisenger was her personal property. Of course, for all Emilia knew, the two of them were intimately involved. She knew that happened a lot in the bigger firms.

"I guess if you don't need me, I'll return to my desk and that complaint I'm finishing up for that suit against the housing authority." Greta smiled at Linc then glared at Emilia.

"I'll be in to review it later. Please make sure we aren't disturbed," Linc said, dismissing his assistant. "And shut the door on your way out."

Greta sniffed loudly as she obeyed her orders.

When she was gone, Emilia indicated the chairs she and Linc had abandoned. "Come and sit."

"Why don't you want me to share any information with Greta? She's my assistant and is used to being involved in every aspect of my practice."

Emilia pulled out her chair and sat. "First of all, this has nothing to do with your practice and, secondly, she is way too nosy for my comfort. In my experience, people who are too curious, too helpful, or too kind are usually fishing for information."

Linc followed suit and sat as well. "That's pretty sad, detective."

"What?"

"That you go through life ascribing ulterior motives to everyone who is kind to you."

She grinned. "I didn't say that."

Linc nodded. "Yes, you did."

"Actually, I was limiting that phrase to my police work. I don't think every nice person on the planet is evil." As soon as she realized what she said, she burst into laughter. "Sorry, that was stupid."

"I seriously doubt that you have any stupidity in you, but tell me this before I die of curiosity, what's the deal with Simon Bolger? What kind of guy is he that you believe he'd lie on the stand and why would he want to see my brother convicted of murder?"

"He probably didn't care that it was Myles going down for the crime."

"Really? That sounds pretty damn cold." Linc reached for the gun again and inspected the area that had been filed off.

"That's the kind of guy he is. You answered your own question. He's a lowlife street criminal who would sell out his own elderly grandmother if the money was right. Someone paid him to say he saw your brother in the alley buying this firearm."

Emilia reached over and tapped it.

Linc set the gun back on the plastic bag. "But what self-respecting prosecutor would put a known liar on the stand?"

She stared at him for a moment without saying a word. Was the man really that naïve? Did he think there were no prosecutors who would do anything for a conviction? If they truly believed a man was guilty, they'd put on any witness who came forward. Not that they would buy testimony themselves but they might not ask too many questions about why the witness was coming forward. No, they'd be more likely to offer a prayer of thanksgiving to God in church on Sunday for bringing forth their necessary witness. Seeing the light dawn on his face made her smile.

He nodded. "Got it. I understand."

"Sorry."

"Where do we go from here?"

"I think we keep at it and look through this box some more then head to your house to look at your notes but I may have to meet you there later. I have somewhere I need to be for part of the afternoon on another case I'm working."

"I hope you won't be in trouble with your captain for spending so much time here this morning."

"No. Howard and I are pretty sure your brother's case ties in to Van Nuys's murder so it won't be a problem."

"Not that I want to remind you of anything that may be a sore subject, but you thought Clifford said my name when he was dying so why do you think you're right about his death being connected to Myles?"

Linc held his hands up as if in surrender as he said the words and said them in a non-confrontational manner as well. Emilia presumed he did it so she wouldn't take it as an attack on her and Howard's investigative prowess.

She grinned. "He still could've been saying your name, you know. We're merely giving you the benefit of the doubt here so we can look at your notes."

"Touché, Detective, touché."

"Next plan of attack after going through this box is to locate Bolger. I've got to tell the guys at the precinct to be on the lookout for that scumbag so we can question him." Emilia glanced around the room and spied the telephone then rethought her first inclination. She pulled out her cell phone. "I'm going to call over and ask the desk sergeant to get a note out to everyone but I'm going outside to use my phone. I don't want anyone to overhear me."

She tilted her head toward the credenza where the office phone sat. It appeared to have about fifteen extensions. She'd never seen a phone with so many buttons. "Do me a favor and don't talk about Myles's case on these phones anymore. To anyone. Okay?"

"You think they're tapped?"

"I have no idea, Linc, but you've had too many people in this building or associated with your family killed on or near these premises. I have a hinky feeling that someone here is either in cahoots with a murderer or has it in for you Eisengers. I'm merely pointing out that you need to be wary of what you say, when you say it, and on what apparatus you say it."

"You'd be a great conspiracy theorist, you know."

"If we find out who killed Van Nuys and it helps release your brother from Angola, you'll be thanking me for my paranoia."

Linc took her hands in his. "Right now, I already am thanking you for what you've done so far. The mere fact that you believe there's a chance to free Myles and that he may have been set up is priceless to me. I've been all alone in this battle for so long, I'm grateful to have someone who has a little faith that we can free him from this hell he's been in and has been bearing with silence and dignity."

Emilia looked down at their hands. His were warm on hers. "I can't promise anything but I'm willing to try."

"And for that, I thank you."

He spoke the words so softly that she glanced up and into his eyes to be sure she heard him. She was shocked to see that tears welled in those deep blue orbs. It was a long moment before she could tear her gaze away.

To cover her embarrassment, she pulled back and clapped her hands together once. "Back to work."

She knew her voice was too bright and fake but she

needed to clear an image out of her head. The one of her kissing him on that lovely mouth that was so close to hers when she was gazing into his eyes. It would have been too easy to capture his lips with hers. She'd never in her life wanted to kiss someone as much as she wanted to kiss him.

☞☜

Linc shook his head when Emilia startled him by clapping her hands. Was he really going to kiss her in the second before she did that? Yesterday, he thought the woman was impossible and today he wanted to kiss her? Surely it was gratitude for the fact that she now believed that Myles had been set up. It couldn't be her cute little nose that crinkled when she smiled or those gorgeous green eyes, could it?

He watched as she moved some of the other plastic evidence bags around. Her hands seemed to be shaking. Had she been as affected by that moment between them as he?

A knock on the door interrupted his thoughts. "Darn it, I told Greta to leave us be. Let me see what she wants now." Linc stood and walked around the table.

Before he arrived at the door, it opened and Howard Mills entered. "How's it going?" Howard asked.

"We're making some progress." Linc glanced down at his watch. "You're right in time for lunch."

"Let's take it to go and head up to see your brother. I hear that the cops up there may have made some progress and I wanted to have a chat with them, too." Howard nodded at Emilia. "Sorry to ditch you again, partner, but you have to meet Amy this afternoon. Captain said to pass the word on to you."

"How's your mom?" Emilia asked.

"It was just heartburn. All the tests came back normal."

"Good, I'm glad she's all right. Must be a relief."

"Yeah. It is but it made for a long night. Speaking of long nights, better get going and catch up with Amy. The sooner you go, the sooner you'll be done.

"You're right. I had better move along. I guess I'll lock this stuff up at the precinct and grab my own lunch before I take off to see her."

"We'll put it all in my trunk. That way it's still in our custody. Pack it up so we can get on the road." Howard strode over to the box and started to reload all the documents and bags of evidence. "I guess Eisenger here can give me an update on our drive."

"Sure. I will." Linc turned to Emilia. "When you get finished with this Amy person, give us a call and, if we're back in the city, we can have a working dinner at my place and you two can check out my notes."

"Sounds good." Emilia replaced the firearm in its bag, sealed it, initialed the sticker, added the date she'd opened the bag, and set it in the box. "I'll be off now."

"We'll call you later. Enjoy your visit with Amy."

Emilia snorted, walked out of the conference room, and shut the door behind her.

"Who's this Amy person that Emilia clearly dislikes?" Linc asked.

"A witness. Amy and Emilia are a lot alike and butt heads a lot. Right now Amy is an integral part of another investigation that we need to wrap so Em will have to deal with her for a while longer."

"Seems to me that your partner butts heads with a lot of people."

"Was she rude today? I'm sorry if she comes across as abrasive. She's a nice gal but right now, she's a sore-tailed bear, as my mamma says. She's trying to prove herself on these cases since she's recently been promoted. She doesn't want the brass to think they made a mistake. Her putting that kind of pressure on herself is making her edgy and cranky."

"She was actually nice today and we worked well together. I think I got to see a little bit behind the mask, so to speak." Linc picked up his jacket off the back of the chair and tugged it on. "Let's get on the road. I'll tell you all about what we found. I wanted to ask you what you know about Simon Bolger, too."

"How'd he come up?" Howard raised his brows.

"I'll tell you in the car. Emilia thinks the walls here have ears. Hand me the box and let's head out."

"I got it if you'll open the door."

Linc opened the conference room door and held it for Howard. He followed him to the elevator. While they waited for it to come, Greta came from down the hallway with a thick file folder in her hands. She called out, "Mr. Eisenger, remember you need to sign those pleadings."

"Does she have a GPS in your coat pocket? How'd she know you were leaving?" Howard whispered.

"I don't know. Hang on." Linc closed the distance between him and his assistant. "Let me see it. We're going out to lunch and you need to get it to the runner service before I get back." He took the folder from her hand and read the document on top. "How'd you know I was leaving?"

"I heard the door close to the conference room." Greta handed him a pen and he signed the pleading.

"Way down there in your office?"

"Yeah." Greta turned red and Linc knew she had to be lying.

Was she spying on him like Emilia thought? He found that hard to believe. She'd been with the firm for a long time. Why would she need to spy on her boss? He shook his head. Paranoia was setting in. How had Emilia been able to plant the idea in his head so quickly that he had enemies in his own firm?

"When will you be back?" Greta asked.

"I'm not sure. I think I have one appointment this afternoon. See if you can move it to right at five. I should be back by then."

"Where are you going? That's a long lunch. It's not like you to blow off your appointments."

He handed her the file. Yeah, she was being pretty nosy. As he thought about it, though, he decided that she really wasn't being more than her usual self. She always needed to know where he was during office hours so she could arrange his schedule.

"I'm not blowing them off. I asked that you to move the *one* I have to five. If it isn't convenient for the client, have the associate assigned to the case—I think it's Melanie, isn't it?—meet with them. She can handle what I need today and then they can see me next time."

"You're not going to tell me where you're going?" Greta's bottom lip quivered.

Lord, was the woman going to cry? What was that about?

"No. I'm going to help the detective. I think he wants me to keep quiet. I'll have my cell. If you need me, call."

"I don't like this, Mr. Eisenger. This is not normal. I'm worried about you. I think the stress of the last few months is affecting you."

"Look, I need to go. Detective Mills is over there holding a heavy box and waiting for me. We'll have this conversation some other time."

Linc turned to walk toward the elevator but he didn't miss the look on her face. It was a combination of hurt, anger, and confusion. Yeah, they needed to have a conversation for sure but not now.

Right now, he wanted to find out what Howard Mills might know about one bad criminal named Simon Bolger.

Chapter 14

The afternoon with Emilia dressed as Amy wore on, long and tedious, and with no progress on the case. At four, Emilia decided to head over to Jackson Square and see what Alyce-Faye was doing. Mondays in October were sometimes slow. Most tourists wanted palm and Tarot readings on the weekends since school was in session and only singles or older people with no children were in the French Quarter area during the early daytime hours. Of course, it was now four p.m. and the kids were out of school so there could be groups of them in the park who might decide to get a reading. Emilia took a chance, anyway, on her friend not being busy.

Deciding that she might be better off strolling as Amy after dark, Emilia approached Alyce-Faye's table where she sat with an array of candles and little marble carvings of animals. She had a space cleared for what

Emilia knew was her favorite deck of cards. She wasn't tied up with a customer and was sitting in her lawn chair watching the crowd.

Alyce-Faye noticed her coming and grinned. "Hey there, lady of the night. Come over and get your palm read. You have some good news in that palm of yours. I can see it from here." It was her standard come-on patter so Emilia knew she wanted her to pretend to be a customer.

"How much?" Emilia asked when she was at the table.

"Twenty dollars. Come. Sit. I will tell you some things about yourself."

"Twenty seems like a lot," Emilia said as she sat one of the lawn chairs in front of the table.

"I know how hard you work for your twenty, so for you, fifteen. Is that fair, lady?" Alyce-Faye leaned forward and whispered, "I have something for you."

"What's that?"

"Hold your hand out so I can be reading it. These people around here watch the competition like crazy. It's like no one wants anyone else to have any business."

"Then wouldn't it be better if they thought I was here as a friend and not a customer?"

"Uh-uh. No. What happens is that, if some tourist sees me doing business with you, they'll think I'm good as I have customers and the others aren't since they don't. I'll end up with a line here."

Emilia grinned. "Then you need to be paying me the fifteen. Sort of like a commission."

"Give me your hand before I swat you." Alyce-Faye reached over and grabbed Emilia's right hand. She ran her index finger across the back. "I'm going to give you the deluxe reading. Both sides." She said that last part loud enough that the people around them could hear her.

"What did you learn today?" Emilia whispered.

"There's a fourteen-year-old runaway who has been trying to keep from turning to the life and she came by here with one of the guys from the beignet shop. He had given her some free for breakfast and, since he knows me and that I'm friends with you, he introduced her to me. She's going to meet you here this evening. She saw something when that girl got beaten the other day. You know, the one in a coma?"

"What time does she want to meet? Does she want to talk to a cop or a hooker?" Emilia sincerely hoped the girl was ready to talk to a cop. True, she'd have to be ready to be sent home to her parents but she had to know if she went to the authorities that they wouldn't let her remain on the streets.

"I didn't tell her that you're a cop. I told her I had a friend who helps girls in trouble and that you knew that girl who got beaten and you were trying to get information to go to the cops with."

"You know I can't let her stay on the streets once I talk to her, right?"

"Ooh, look, lady, your love life is getting ready to take a turn for the better," Alyce-Faye said loudly.

"Why are you changing the subject?" Emilia hissed under her breath.

An almost-imperceptible nod in the direction of the next booth over told Emilia what she needed to know. Someone was listening.

"Really?" Emilia snorted aloud. "Kind of interesting since I really don't have a love life. I have a *sex* life but not a love life."

The woman at the next booth snickered. "I guess she told you, Alyce-Faye."

"No, really, Magdalina, come and look." Alyce-Faye held Emilia's hand out toward the other woman.

The woman rose and strolled over. She took Emilia's hand in hers and studied it a few moments. "Hmm. That really is odd, isn't it? Have you thought about leaving the life?" she asked Emilia.

How to answer the woman? Since she wasn't really in the life of a hooker, what should she say? It suddenly dawned on her. "Actually, yes, that's kind of why I wanted my palm read. I was wondering if I could make a clean break and find another way to make a living."

"If what we're seeing in your hand is any indication—and we have to believe it since that's what we do—you're going to find true love and be very happy." The woman winked. "And quite soon."

"Great. Now do I have to pay you both?" Emilia put a fake pout on her face.

"No. That was my gift to you." Magdalina bowed and returned to her seat.

As she sat, a woman in red accompanied by a man in khaki pants and a white shirt walked over to her. "Will you read my palm? I heard what you said to that girl and I want mine read, too."

Alyce-Faye nodded. "See? What'd I tell you?"

"That was probably your customer. I should move away."

"No problem." Alyce-Faye waved her hand. "There will be more." She dropped her voice again. "You come back tonight at nine p.m. The girl will meet you at the statue of Andrew Jackson. She has a denim coat with a big pink peace sign embroidered on the back of it. Okay?"

"I'll be here but I'm going to have to call her parents when we're done."

"I'll leave that to you but you need to come as Amy. I told her what you'd have on, too."

"Geez. I'm going to be in and out of these clothes all day long."

Alyce-Faye laughed. "Of course you will, you crazy thing, you're a hooker."

"Very funny—not." Emilia stood. She dug some money out of her back pocket and handed it over to Alyce-Faye. "Thanks."

She turned and walked away. She knew she'd somehow get the money back. Her friend would bring her breakfast again or maybe splurge on her favorite wine as a gift. Alyce-Faye never took money from her pals. She thought it would go against her karma points if she did and, besides, it wasn't a real reading anyway. Or was it? Emilia shook her head. The other reader said something about her love life too, didn't she? Well, that didn't make it real, though. That Magdalina and Alyce-Faye probably backed each other up all the time. Reinforced the reading, so to speak.

She shrugged as she headed back to the precinct. She was going to clean up and meet Linc and Howard before she had to return to the park at nine.

On her way to the precinct, she saw the man in gold, Adam Pipersburg. Making a decision, she strolled over to where he was packing up his gear. "Hey there. Did you make any money today?"

"Not much. How about you?" He grinned. He knew her of course. She used to walk the beat in the area before she was promoted and he knew she was undercover as Amy, too since she'd had to ask him about things he'd seen around the square before.

"Just working toward my pension."

"A lofty goal indeed. What can I do for you today—" He lowered his voice. "—Officer?"

"I'm on the lookout for Simon Bolger. Have you seen him around lately?"

"Maybe a week or so ago but not since then."

"If you see him, call me immediately. Do you still have my card?"

"I do. In fact, I have your number in my phone. What did ole Simon do now?"

"I need to ask him some questions. Don't let him know I'm looking for him, okay?"

"Sure thing. If I see him, I'll let you know." Adam picked up his duffle bag and box he stood on while performing. "I'm headed to the showers and then to get a cold beer. Want to come?"

"I can't. Still on duty." Emilia ran her hand up and down her side. "Can't you tell?"

He laughed. "Hard to know. You're definitely one sexy mama in those shorts."

"Yeah, me and my flat chest."

Adam winked. "Some guys like that."

She grinned. "Get out of here with your craziness and remember to call me if you see anyone in particular."

"Yes, ma'am. Enjoy your evening. Make lots of money. For your pension." He left, whistling a tune as he went.

Emilia returned to the precinct to find Howard waiting for her with news from the warden at Angola.

⁂

Lincoln made it back to his office in time to meet

with his clients along with the associate, Melanie. The meeting lasted until after six. He called Howard Mills as soon as he was done and offered to pick up a pizza and salad for them to eat while they met at his place to go through his notes. Greta had retrieved that transcript of the trial from the investigator and he would be bringing that to his house as well. Howard agreed to the dinner plans but told him that Emilia would have to leave before nine as she had an appointment then.

Curious about the after-hours appointment, although he knew most detectives didn't work nine to five, Linc found himself wondering if Emilia had a boyfriend or lover. He's noticed she didn't wear a ring but that might not mean anything since she may leave it at home while on duty. He knew a few women in law enforcement who did that. Linc shook his head. Why would it matter to him if the woman had a man in her life? They didn't have one thing in common and it was none of his business.

He picked up the phone to order the pizza and found himself reliving that moment when he almost kissed her.

"Stop it man. You're losing it. She is nothing like your type." He keyed in the number to his favorite Italian place, a little café near his house called Nero's Fiddle.

When Nick, the owner, answered, Linc placed an order for two large pizzas and three Italian salads with Nick's secret recipe dressing—a tangy, delightful taste sensation on the tongue. Linc asked him to add an extra container of the dressing since he loved to dip his pizza in it as well. After indicating that he'd pick up the order to go, Linc hung up and packed his briefcase.

He wasn't the last to leave the office by any means. There were still a number of associates hard at work, trying to prove themselves partner material. Of course, now that Van Nuys was gone, the real estate department was in a flux and the other partners needed to meet and decide who would either be moved up to supervise the department or if they would need to hire someone with more experience from outside the firm.

He shrugged off that worry for another day and headed to the elevator. Oddly, he was surprised not to run into Greta. She seemed to be everywhere he went these days and he knew she hadn't gone home yet. He made his escape without seeing her and exited through the main doors after signing out with the security man on duty.

He didn't see anyone he knew on the way to his car but he vowed to return to the area after his meeting with the two detectives since it would be a good time to see if he could find that young girl prostitute. He wasn't going to give up on helping her if he could. He laughed slightly as he thought about her aversion to him littering on the street. There was still something about her that bothered him but he couldn't pin it down.

After the stop at Nero's Fiddle to pick up dinner, he made it to his driveway right about the same time as the detectives.

He idly wondered if they'd been following him but

guessed that they'd probably timed their arrival from the phone call to Howard.

Linc stepped out of his car and walked around to the passenger side to get the food.

Emilia moved in behind him. "Need some help?"

He handed her the bag with the three salads. "Here, take these. I'll grab the pizzas."

"Man, those smell divine. What kind did you get?" she asked as she and Howard followed him to the front door.

"I wasn't sure so I played it safe and got one pepperoni and then I went all out and got Nick's special pizza called Rome's Burning."

"What's on that one?" Howard asked. "I'm kind of afraid to ask."

"It's got spicy salami, a smattering of anchovies, jalapenos, and hot sauce. It also has oregano and banana peppers."

Howard laughed. "In other words, a mouthful of fire and heartburn."

"It's my favorite and I figured if you both hated it, I'd have leftovers for lunch tomorrow." Linc opened the door and let the others past him.

"It sounds good to me. I can't wait to try it." Emilia laughed. "I'm a pizza for breakfast kind of girl, though. My leftovers never make it to lunchtime."

Linc led them into the kitchen and placed the pizzas on the table. "Set the salads here and I'll get some plates.

I have beer in the fridge. I also have tea or water. What'll it be?"

"No beer for us. We're still working," Howard said. "Why don't you tell me where the plates are and I'll get those while you grab your files? Save some time since Em has to leave early."

"Sure. They're in the cabinet over there." Linc pointed across to the upper shelves next to the sink. "Glasses are in the next one over. I'll have to go back to my car and get the transcript. I got that returned to me."

Emilia held her hand out. "Give me your keys and I'll go get that."

Linc pulled his key ring from his pocket and passed them to her.

When they all returned from their tasks, Howard had the table set. Emilia walked in turning pages in the transcript.

"What are you trying to find?" Linc asked as he sat his voluminous file on the table and took his seat.

"Exhibit twenty-three. I want to see what that missing exhibit was but it doesn't seem like the lawyer went in order." She flipped more pages as she scanned them.

"Here," Linc reached for the transcript. "Let me show you something." He turned to the back of the volume he held. "See how the court reporter has a summary of the testimony here? It's sometimes faster to look here." He ran his finger down the page and flipped to the next one.

"Not there either." Emilia turned the page. "I'm a fast reader."

"I see that." Linc smiled at her and she returned the look with a grin that almost took his breath away. He inhaled a sharp gasp. She was gorgeous when she was happy. He guessed he hadn't noticed it because she always seemed guarded and had on her cop-face. He tore his gaze away from hers with effort and stared at the page.

She flipped to the next one and, in a moment, said, "Found it."

"What was the exhibit?" Howard asked as he chewed on his piece of pepperoni pizza.

"Page forty-three." Emilia turned to that page. "Here's the witness identifying the document. He says, "This is the original trust agreement entered into in the 1840s. It sets up the initial trust on the properties. It's been updated since then, of course, but this is the original."

"Who is the witness?" Howard asked.

Emilia and Linc answered at the same time, "Clifford Van Nuys."

Emilia gasped and gaped at Linc. "How did you know? I just read it here on the page."

"I was in that trial every minute, Emilia. I remembered Clifford saying that as you read it right now."

"But why didn't you tell us Van Nuys was one of the witnesses in Myles's case? Didn't you think that was important?" Emilia was standing now. "This is big, Linc.

Big. If you'd told us Van Nuys was a witness in Myles's case that first night when he was found dead, it may have changed our investigation."

"Now wait a second. That first night I had no idea that the two things could be related at all. That would've been a big leap for me to take. Van Nuys testified because he was a real estate lawyer not because he saw anything the night that man was killed. The prosecution called him to identify documents found on the victim."

"So this trust from the 1840s was in the possession of the decedent?" Howard asked. "Did they give great significance to that? Did the prosecution say that was somehow tied to any motive Myles might have to kill the man—not that I'm saying that Myles did it—I'm merely trying to see what the purpose of the testimony of Clifford Van Nuys would have been."

"I don't think they focused overmuch on Van Nuys. They really spun the whole thing as a dispute between two men over a woman. That never set right with me since Myles wasn't involved with anyone at the time. We couldn't figure it out. Myles and I, as well as his defense attorney, discussed it over and over." Linc shook his head and sat down. He pulled his plate toward him and, taking a slice of pizza, put it to his mouth. "It was odd, that's all. I don't know why that guy had a copy of the trust on him when he died. Myles and I haven't really discussed that because we keep focusing on the woman and what they said about him and her being an item. Myles denies it."

"We're going to have to study that document, Linc. Can you get a copy of it? The fact that it's missing from the evidence box is very telling to me." Emilia sat. "Let's eat and then get going on the other stuff."

"I can get a copy of the trust. It's in the safe at the office. I also imagine there's a copy at the house my mother inherited from Dad when he died." Linc chewed his pizza.

"You don't seem to get along with your mother, why is that?" Emilia asked after she swallowed a bite.

"Is this an interrogation, Detective?"

"Nope. Just curiosity." She looked over at Howard. "Tell the man how nosy I am."

Howard laughed. "Lord, woman, that would take all day and we don't have that long. It's soon going to be time for you to go."

They finished their meal and after clearing the table, Linc opened his file folder. "What do you want to see now?"

Chapter 15

Twenty minutes before time for her Amy persona to meet the fourteen-year-old girl, Emilia and Howard stood in Linc's driveway getting into their police-issue sedan. They hadn't made any more progress with the case but Howard was going to take the other part of the files that they hadn't gotten through home with him and study them overnight.

Emilia opened her car door and addressed Lincoln. "We have to question Michael Rhodes in the morning. He was up at Angola for the rodeo and he also was seen in the Quarter around the time of the other case we're investigating so we won't be able to catch up with you until later in the day."

"That's all right. I have some depositions tomorrow that will last most of the day and I also have to set a partner's meeting so I'll be pretty tied up myself." Linc shook her hand. "I'll touch base when I'm free and we'll see what you two are doing about that time."

"Sounds like a plan." Howard tossed the files onto the seat and climbed in on the driver's side.

As soon as they cleared Eisenger's driveway, Emilia reached behind her seat and pulled her Amy costume into her lap. She shimmied her jeans off and slipped into the shorts, then tugged her long-sleeve T-shirt over her head to trade for the half shirt Amy wore.

"Never mind me over here, Em. Just go ahead and change clothes."

"You've seen women in bathing suits with less on. We all have the same parts. I've never understood that whole being modest thing. Besides, we don't have time to return to the precinct for me to change. I need to be dropped off at the park to meet this girl." She looked at her watch. "Like now. I don't want to be late and give her a chance to get spooked and run."

"I know, I know. I'm driving as fast as I can. By the way, good try on the attempt to draw Eisenger out on his relationship with his mother."

"I *did* try but you sure didn't help. You had to remind us that we were running out of time. What was that all about?" Emilia pulled the hated red wig on over her hair.

"I'm sorry. I realized it as soon as I said the words."

"Rookie."

"Hey. That's a horrible insult." Howard guffawed and pulled into the lane alongside Jackson Square where the horse-drawn carriages waited for riders. "Get out here and I'll park. I'll be right over to be your backup if you need me."

"Thanks. It shouldn't be necessary but it's good to know you'll be there." She opened the door and stepped out.

Strolling through the park, toward the statue in the middle, Emilia noticed a girl in a denim jacket and jeans pacing around the base of the statue. She made a beeline for the girl when she saw the pink peace sign on the back of the coat. She sauntered along with her hips rolling.

When she reached the girl, Emilia said, "Hey. I'm Amy. My friend Alyce-Faye, the psychic, said you wanted to talk to me about something?" Emilia did her best to keep her voice even and smooth. It wouldn't do to get the girl rattled.

"Hi. I'm Roberta—I mean Bobbi. I'm from Minnesota and I'm scared. I ran away from home and don't want to go back but I need help. Some of the ladies I met said you might be able to find me a way out. There's this man who wants to put me on the street to work as a hooker but I don't want to do that."

"Come and sit with me. Let's go." Emilia took Bobbi by the arm and led her to one of the benches under the magnolia trees at the edge of the park.

As soon as they were seated, Emilia asked, "What did the ladies tell you about me?"

"Just that you knew some of the business owners here and that you might be able to find me a real job.

They also said you were trying to assist some of their friends who'd been hurt." The girl looked Emilia up and down. "Looks to me like you need help yourself. When did you last eat?"

It was all Emilia could do not to laugh. The poor girl had come all the way from Minnesota, had been living on the streets, and was worried about whether Emilia had eaten or not. It was endearing and a little bit crazy. "I'm fine. In fact, I was going to suggest that we share a muffuletta." She pulled out some money. "I can pay."

"Wow. Sure. I've never had one but I've heard of them."

"Let's talk about what you wanted to tell me and then we'll walk over to City Grocery. They're right down the street and they have the best ones in town. The olive salad they use is divine."

"Okay." Bobbi glanced around. "I'm a little scared to talk out here in the open like this. I don't know who might hear us."

"They're going to lock the park gates in a bit, anyway. We can go over by the entrance to Pirates Alley. It's sheltered there and we can stand with our backs to the wall. No one can sneak up on us there." Emilia stood and offered her hand to Bobbi.

As they strolled toward Pirates Alley, Bobbi suddenly grabbed Emilia's arm. "Wait. Stop."

"What?" Emilia glanced about, glad to see Howard had come around the corner and seen the direction she was walking. She nodded almost imperceptibly at him to encourage him to follow along.

"See that woman over there?" Bobbi tilted her head in the direction of the cafe on the corner. Emilia could see a red-haired woman dressed in a blue tracksuit who was facing the other way.

"Yes. What about her?"

"I've seen her around the Quarter. She's been questioning all the street people and she was near the girl who was beaten right before it happened. She scares me. I saw her talking to that young hooker-girl not five or ten minutes before the girl got beaten up. I also heard from someone else that the same woman knew that lawyer who was killed the other day."

Emilia tightened her grip on Bobbi's arm. "She what?"

"I don't know if that part's true, but that's the word on the street."

Emilia was determined to get a look at the woman's face. "Stay right here. Let me take a peek at her and see if I know who she is."

Bobbi backed up three steps. "I'm afraid."

Emilia glanced behind her and summoned Howard. "Here's a friend of mine. His name is Howard. You can trust him. He'll wait right here with you, okay?"

"I don't know." The girl was actually shivering in fear.

Howard touched the girl's shoulder. "Em—uh,

Amy—will be right back. I promise you'll be fine. Stay here with me."

Emilia nodded to Howard. "I'm going to check that lady out. Keep an eye on Bobbi here for me."

"Go."

Emilia was glad that Howard didn't ask questions. Maybe he had confidence in her abilities or trusted that she'd explain when she returned. Those thoughts made her braver and she stood straighter. She sauntered casually toward the woman in the tracksuit determined to see if she recognized her from the front. Even though Bobbi wasn't sure if the word on the street was true and that the woman was involved in some way in Emilia's cases, Emilia's gut told her this was an important moment.

Before she could see the woman's face, she noticed Lincoln Eisenger coming toward her. Crap, crap, crap what was he doing down here? She panicked slightly but decided she could turn around and he wouldn't realize it was her. Torn about what to do, she stopped short.

After a heartbeat or two, the woman in the tracksuit turned her head toward Emilia who recognized her in that moment. It was the woman who'd staggered out of the building where the Eisenger firm was located. She'd been the one who Howard and Emilia thought was drunk the day Van Nuys was found dead. The one who hadn't signed in with security.

As soon as Emilia placed who she was, she glanced over at Howard and widened her eyes. The next split-second after that, the woman in the tracksuit took off at a run. Emilia kicked into gear and chased after her. They ran down Pirates Alley and deeper into the French Quarter. Emilia struggled a bit in her high-heeled boots. She pulled her radio out of her pocket and called in to dispatch for backup. She panted as she tried to keep the dispatcher apprised of the direction she was running.

Winded and about to give up because she kept twisting her ankle and almost losing her balance, Emilia became aware that there was someone following her. She heard the thudding of feet behind her. She hoped it was another law enforcement officer but she didn't want to slow down to find out.

The woman disappeared around a corner. Emilia almost lost her. She kept talking into her radio. Relieved when the dispatcher let her know that there were officers on foot coming from the other direction, Emilia slowed down a bit so she could catch a deep breath. She had a stitch in her side, too.

She wanted to question this woman but she knew she'd never outrun her in the blasted boots. As soon as Emilia caught her breath, she increased her pace again. In a few steps, though, whoever was trailing her caught up and was suddenly beside her. Emilia chanced a glance over to see who it was and let out a gasp. Lincoln Eisenger was running in sync with her.

His eyes widened and he reached out for her arm. Emilia found some reserve of strength and kicked it up a notch. She moved past him, still on the radio.

The dispatcher came on to let her know the woman had been apprehended and was enroute to the precinct in the custody of two patrolmen.

Emilia stopped running. She leaned her hands on her knees and spent a few moments catching her breath.

When she looked up, Linc, dead serious, said, "I knew those freckles on your nose were familiar. What the hell are you doing, Detective Hammond?"

❧

Linc couldn't believe it. He'd had an entire conversation with Emilia when she was dressed as this hooker persona and yet he'd never tied it together that they were the same person. How had this slipped past him? He who prided himself on his powers of observation?

He followed along beside Emilia as she stalked down the sidewalk. He kept giving her sidelong glances. Stunned that the girl he thought was about fourteen was actually Emilia Hammond, Linc couldn't stop looking at her.

"Will you cut it out already," Emilia said.

"What?"

"Stop staring at me out of the corner of your eye like that. It's me. Get over it." As the word *it* came out of her mouth, the heel of her boot broke. "Well, hell's bells, can this night *get* any better?" She hobbled on and Linc couldn't help but laugh at her. "What's so funny, mister?" She stopped and faced him with her hands on her hips. "Why were you chasing me anyway? You were clearly stunned to see it was me when you got beside me so you had to have some other motive for taking off after me when I ran."

"I thought you were a child prostitute—"

"Wait." Emilia held up her right hand. "Just as I was starting to like you, I find out you're some kind of pervert?"

"You *like* me?" He couldn't help it. His heart soared in his chest. The woman liked him.

"Quit grinning like a baboon. You must have missed that whole comment about being a pervert. The Lincoln Eisenger I met last week would've taken my head off for that."

"Ahh, but see, this is a totally different Lincoln Eisenger."

"Lord, I don't have time for this crap. I have to get back to the precinct to question that woman and I also have a runaway from Minnesota to deal with. I can't be screwing around with you right now. Walk and talk. Come on. It's at least fifteen blocks back to where I left Howard. Tell me what your motive was to chase a person who you thought was an underage hooker."

Emilia having obviously forgotten her boot was broken, tried to walk away. She ended up hobbling instead.

Linc laughed again as he followed behind. His spirits

seemed lighter than they had been in months. "Will you have time later?"

"Time for what? You need to answer my question now, not later."

"Time to screw around with me."

She glanced back over her shoulder with a priceless expression. "*What* did you say?"

"You said you didn't have time to screw around with me now. I was merely inquiring if you'd have time later." Linc hoped the look on his face was innocent but he was dead serious as he realized he really did want this woman in his bed. Sooner rather than later.

Emilia kept walking with the up and down steps that her broken boot forced her to do. She turned her head forward and said, "Stop fooling around and tell me why you chased me. Don't make me arrest you."

As much as he enjoyed the view of her from behind, he caught up to walk beside her. "Do you want me to carry you?"

She shook her head. "Why would you even remotely think that I'd want you to carry me?"

"We could make better progress toward the station if you'd let me. You probably don't weigh ninety pounds. I can move faster toting you than you can in those boots."

"Hang on then."

He stopped when she did. She held on to his arm to keep her balance and—one at a time, as she stood on first one leg and then the other—she tugged off the boots.

When she was barefooted, she shoved the boots at him.

"Here. Tote these, *Mr. I Want to Carry Stuff.*"

"You're going to freeze. It *is* October, you know."

"Yeah, it's October in New Orleans. It's still pretty warm out here, or hadn't you noticed?"

"I noticed." He didn't want to say that he'd also noticed her sexy legs. She was short but, man, her legs seemed to go on forever, especially in those short shorts. "It does seem to me that walking these nasty streets barefooted is not a good plan. You have no idea what's on them."

"I'd bet on stale beer, vomit, and old cigarette butts which reminds me of the first time we met. You were smoking and actually littered the butt onto the street, but I haven't seen you smoke since then. What's that about?"

"Come on. I know you need to get back. While we walk, I'll tell you about a dream that Myles and I had before he went to prison and, in the process, you'll learn why I was chasing a young hooker as well as why I was pretending to be a smoker. How's that sound?"

"Sounds like what I wanted to hear in the first place. How it took so long to get to that, I don't know. You lawyers and all the words you have to say drive me crazy."

"Listen to some more of my words, okay? After all, you don't have anything better to do as you walk back to Jackson Square, do you?"

"Not really although a little peace and quiet never hurt anyone."

"I can give you that, too, if you'd prefer."

"Nope. I want to know if you're a menace to society and a pedophile first." Emilia cursed and grabbed her foot.

"What?" Linc asked.

"I stepped on an acorn or something."

"My offer to carry you still stands."

She turned and continued to walk. "You know I might take you up on that if I didn't think you were some sicko that wanted to hire an underage hooker."

"Okay, okay. Here's the deal. Myles and I have this family trust and it owns a lot of real estate—some pretty significant parcels, too. We were planning to set up an assistance center in one of the properties—we'd already talked to the public departments dealing with runaways and were laying the groundwork for a facility where they could find assistance. We planned to get it approved as an orphanage, as well, since so many of these kids would be sent back to awful environments if they were caught. Right now, most get shipped home and some of their homes are worse than the streets."

Linc took hold of Emilia's elbow. "We were well on our way to approval when Myles was arrested. When I saw you dressed as you are—I presume this is the Amy that Howard says you hate—my desire to do the right thing by these kids was reignited. For the first time since

Myles was hauled in for that murder, I actually wanted to get back to our project. I first saw you a few days before Van Nuys died and then I started to pretend to smoke so I'd have a chance to stand on the street and watch for you. I wanted to chat with an underage runaway and see if she'd want to help me with getting the final approval— you know, testify for the benefits of such a facility. I had even gone so far as to set up a meeting to try to get the approval rushed through."

When he was finished with his speech, Emilia came to a standstill. With her opposite hand she took hold of the hand he still had on her elbow. "Dear God, man. Do you hear yourself?"

"What? I don't follow. What do you mean?"

She faced him. "I thought you were supposed to be smart. Think about what you just said to me. How much property are we talking about in that trust? Is it down-town? Is there a lot of income produced from the rentals? Who would stand to gain if you and Myles were out of the way? Where would the money go?"

Linc stared at her for a few seconds, "That's a lot of questions, lady."

"Think about what you said and what I asked." Emilia stood with her arms crossed and watched him.

He stood still and replayed his side of the conversation in his head with her questions in mind. When he'd done so, he smacked himself upside the forehead. "Holy smokes. It's the motive for everything, including Myles being in prison, isn't it? There's a massive fortune at stake here. Dear God, I need to get my hands on that original trust and see where the money goes if something happens to me and my brother."

"Yes, you do." Emilia nodded. "And you need to be careful not to be the next victim."

Chapter 16

Seated across the table from the red-haired woman—who was named Ambrosia Hicks, of all things—Emilia grilled her about the day Van Nuys was killed.

The red wig sat beside Emilia on the table and Howard was on the other side of the wig. Ambrosia glared at them both from her seat on the opposite side of the table. She faced the one-way mirror that allowed the captain and others to watch the interrogation without the witness being aware that she was being observed.

"Tell me again what you were doing in that building last Thursday afternoon. I find it hard to believe that you accidently staggered in there when you were drunk." Emilia knew the woman was lying when she made that her cover story. No way would she have run away this evening if she were innocent and intoxicated at the time of Van Nuys' death.

"That's the truth. I don't know why you don't believe me."

"You ran as soon as you saw me near Pirates Alley. Why would you run from a cop if you hadn't done anything?"

"I hate to break it to you lady but when I saw you coming toward me, I didn't think you were a cop. You looked like a whore to me."

The woman had a point. Emilia forgot she'd initially seen the woman the day Van Nuys died dressed in her own slacks and shirt not in Amy's clothes. Well, damn. What was she thinking? Ambrosia hadn't run from a cop, she'd run from a hooker. Emilia barely refrained from smacking herself. She berated herself for being stupid and bone-headed. How had she not remembered she wasn't Amy when she ran into this woman the first time? Maybe she needed to rest a little. She'd been going non-stop for days, trying to prove her worth to the department, and she really wasn't sure she even cared anymore. It was too hard. All she wanted to do at the moment was put her head down and cry.

Emilia turned to Howard. "Can you take over here for a moment? I need to get some coffee. I'll be right back."

Howard gave her a look that she knew meant he wasn't sure what the game was. She usually didn't leave an interrogation unless they were trying to play the witness or suspect in some manner. This time is was all about self-preservation. Emilia was going to lose it and she didn't want to do it in the stationhouse.

She stood and left the room. As she headed down the stairs to the exit with her head down, the captain called out behind her, "Detective Hammond?"

"Yes?"

"Has something happened?"

"I've thought of something I need to do. I'll be right back." Emilia was terrified that she'd never make it outside.

"Hurry up. I don't know what can be more important right now than this witness and then dealing with the runaway who has refused to give us the information on her parents. We need you here to take care of these things, Emilia."

"I know. I know." Emilia waved her hand over her head, clattered the rest of the way down the stairs, and fled outside. She darted around the corner and, hunching over, she sobbed into her hands for a few seconds. The tears flowed through her fingers and dripped onto the ground.

When she'd gained control of herself, she stood and nearly jumped out of her skin when she noticed the shadow looming over her.

Her eyes adjusted and she recognized the man. "Sheesh, Linc, you scared me."

"You scared me first." He stepped forward and enveloped her in his embrace. He really was a lot taller than her. She hadn't quite realized it until he was standing thigh-to-thigh with her.

"What do you mean, I scared you first?" Her voice was muffled as her face was smashed into his chest.

He reached between them and lifted her chin with his index finger until she was looking him in the eyes. "I never thought I'd see the marvelous Emilia Hammond break down and doubt herself. I thought you to be invincible and incredibly clever and it surprised me to find that you actually let some self-doubt creep in."

"I *am* human you know. Not some kind of cyborg."

"You had me fooled when I first met you. I thought you were some kind of tough woman who never got rattled, but now I know the real you and guess what? I quite like the more human version I just met."

Emilia pulled her face away from his fingertips. "How did you find me here, anyway?"

"I followed you out of the precinct. I was sitting downstairs with your friend from Minnesota having a chat with her as she waited to talk to you next. When I saw you dash by, I realized that you were about to lose it. I wanted to be there to make it easier on you, or to guard you, if someone else came by to witness your breakdown."

"How could you know that?"

"I think I can read you by now."

She opened her mouth to comment on that remark but, before she could make a sound, he leaned in and captured her lips with his. His were soft and gentle as he explored hers. No other man had treated her as gently and more tears welled at the corners of her eyes.

In a few moments, Linc pulled away and smiled down at her. "I want to do that for a lot longer but I heard your captain tell you to get back soon so I better let you go."

"Thank you for helping calm me. I was making a fool of myself in there and I needed to clear my head." She wasn't sure her head was actually clear, since the kiss was pretty spectacular, but she did feel calmer than she had when she ran out.

"You're welcome. Let's head back inside and you go kick some butt. I'll hang out with Bobbi until you're ready for her. She's a good kid and she's exactly the kind of person Myles and I wanted to help with our idea. She has a horrific family life and I think it would be a crime for her to have to return to it."

Emilia passed him on her way back to the precinct. "We have to do what the government requires, Linc. I'm going to talk to her as a witness and I'll be able to hold her here for a few days but, chances are, she'll have to go home. I hate it as much as you do but that's the normal protocol."

"Let's see what we can do about that later."

They came around the corner to the entrance to the station. "I thought you were going to get that trust document for us to review. What happened?"

"We've waited this long, I figured it would keep another day, or at least until tomorrow morning—" Linc glanced down at his watch. "—which is in about six hours from now."

"You know what you could do for me?"

"What's that?"

"Help me find a place for Bobbi to stay tonight. I'm surprised the captain hasn't called in the child protective services yet. I asked him to wait since I thought we'd get to question her pretty soon. Now it looks like it's going to be a while with that Ambrosia woman unless Howard made progress while I was gone. I'd hate to see Bobbi placed in a home where she might take off before we can help her. She seems awfully skittish."

"She was really upset when she got here, I know that. She thought she could trust you and you ended up being the very thing she was trying to avoid."

"I know." Emilia opened the door and entered the building. She nodded at Bobbi who was seated on a bench by the desk sergeant and spoke to her. "I'll be back. Don't worry."

Linc stepped over to Bobbi and sat beside her. "I'm going to wait with you. I'm going to be your lawyer so you're safe with me." He pulled out his cell phone. "I'm making some calls to see if I can find a place for you to stay until they can question you."

Emilia moved out of hearing then but she knew Linc wouldn't let her down. She touched her lips with her first two fingers and relived the kiss. The man really was a divine kisser.

At the top of the stairs stood the captain and Howard. Howard stepped forward. "Good plan, partner. As soon as you were out of the room, that chick spilled her guts. I don't think she would've ever said anything worth hearing if you hadn't left. She clearly didn't want to wait around for you to come back."

"What did she say?" Emilia asked.

"She was there at the law firm's building without permission. It seems she was under the security desk providing a service to the guard on duty when Van Nuys staggered in with the gunshot wound. According to her, he poked at the elevator button until the car arrived. The guard kept trying to get him to sign in but Van Nuys kept muttering something about a link to the real estate."

"There's the link word that the receptionist mentioned," Emilia said. "What else did Ambrosia offer? Did she say why she ran from me?"

"Something about having gotten into an argument with a group of prostitutes about cadging their johns—invading their territory. She said the look on your face when you made eye contact with her made her think you were going to whip her butt for being with that security guard and others on that street. It seems she was the one they all called—cheaper, faster service—all the guards on that block shared her number." Howard laughed. "Hooker's running sales, who would've thought?"

"Good Lord, what's next?" the captain asked.

"Next we have to deal with that child downstairs, sir." Emilia pointed to the floor.

"Can we call child services and handle her issues in the morning? I held off because you asked me to but it's really late now and that kid needs to be in a bed."

"I'm taking her with me. I've signed on to be her pro bono counsel and I've got a place for her to stay." Linc and Bobbi had arrived at the top of the stairs and Linc addressed the captain. "I've talked to a case worker for the state and she's faxing some paperwork over for you and me to sign."

"I'm not sure how kosher this is, Mr. Eisenger, but I'm so tired that, if the paperwork is in order, I'm all for going home to bed and picking this back up tomorrow. Let's go see if those papers are here." The captain strode to the door of his office.

Howard followed the captain. "Let me go."

Emilia turned to Linc. "Where did you find for her to stay?"

He grinned. "My place."

"Uh-uh." She shook her head. "No way. This is a fourteen-year-old girl. She's not staying in a thirty-year-old man's Garden District mansion alone with said man."

Linc's grin widened. "You're right, she's not."

"Then what's happening?"

"There's this female detective I know who volunteered to stay over, too."

Emilia stood with her hands on her hips. "Who's that? Do I know her?"

"I believe you do. Her name is Emilia although she sometimes goes by Amy." Linc winked as Bobbi cracked up and bent over double in laughter.

∽∾∽

Later, at Linc's house—when Bobbi had been dressed in some of Emilia's pajamas, that they'd popped by her apartment to get, and sent to bed—Emilia and Linc sat on his back patio in the slightly cooler breeze. Emilia soaked her feet in a tub of hot water that he'd provided for her. The soles of her feet had gotten torn up and nasty dirty when she walked back to the precinct barefoot. The hot water that Linc had dumped some sort of scented liquid into was acting as a sedative on her.

Her eyes threatened to close but she was determined to discuss one more thing with him before she turned in. She'd taken a few moments in private with Howard before leaving the station to see if he thought it was the right time to discuss the information that the warden at Angola had shared with them. He'd agreed that it was, since they were now quite sure that Linc had nothing to do with any murder and, most likely, neither did his brother.

Emilia glanced over at Linc where he sat looking absolutely dashing and handsome. How he kept exactly the right amount of scruff on his face all day and all night was a mystery to her but the stuff sure tantalized her.

Linc smiled. His grin was devastating. "What are you doing?"

Even though he'd only kissed her once, and within the last few hours, her opinion of him had changed yet again in that short time. Sure, she'd thought him handsome almost from the moment they'd met—even when he was being a jerk and littering the streets—but he'd had an arrogance about him that was a little off-putting. Now that she knew how gentle he could be and also as softhearted as he was about runaway children, she admired him—almost too much. It was kind of scary.

"Emilia, I asked what you're doing. You're staring at me as if I were going to leap out of this chair and devour you."

"Maybe that would be all right—depending on what you mean by devour, of course." She smiled and glanced down at her hands. Was she being too forward?

Linc moved his chair closer to hers and reached out for her hand. "I have to tell you, Emilia, I would absolutely adore making love to you but, right this moment, I don't think that's a good idea."

"Because Bobbi is upstairs?"

He nodded. "Exactly."

She knew that was the reason, because he'd been so concerned about the girl he wouldn't want to set a bad example for her if she woke. That made Emilia's heart warm even more toward him. Taking a deep breath, she stared into Linc's eyes. "I need to talk to you about something that I've known about for a while but couldn't mention until Howard and I agreed that the time was right." Emilia quite enjoyed the sensations coursing through her at the touch of his hand but decided she needed to let go in order to have this conversation.

"What is it? I don't like the expression on your face. It's pretty serious. You and Howard don't still think I'm involved in any of this, do you?"

"Not anymore. We're both fully convinced that you're in the clear."

"Then why drop my hand and why the odd look on your face?"

"What I'm going to say may cause you some consternation and heartache—"

"Wait, is Myles okay?"

"Yes. He's fine but this *does* have to do with him in a way." Emilia took Linc's hand again. "And you."

"What is it? You're scaring me."

"You know that medical records are privileged, right?"

"Ye—e—es?" Linc dragged the word out into three syllables with a question mark at the end.

"With Myles being in prison, the state stands in loco parentis with him. You know about that too, right?"

"I'm familiar with the concept that the state is in the position of a parent to the inmate." Linc squeezed Emilia's hand. "If you know something about Myles's medical condition, tell me. I promise I won't sue for any violations of the privacy act."

Emilia barked a laugh. "That was not my concern at all, you crazy man, thinking like a lawyer."

"Then what? What's the concern?"

"I've found out tonight how sensitive of a person you are and I don't want to be the one to hurt you."

"You won't hurt me unless you tell me that you won't let me kiss you again someday." He lifted her hand to his mouth and kissed her knuckles.

She removed her hand from his, even though she really wanted him to hold it forever. "This is serious, Lincoln Eisenger. Quit fooling around."

"Then tell me already, Detective Hammond. The sooner you tell me, the sooner I can deal with it. We've already established that it's a medical thing and that it has to do with my brother and maybe me as well."

"Are you cross-examining me, counselor?"

"If that's what it takes to get you to talk, then yeah, I am."

"Fine, fine, fine." Emilia held her hands up in surrender. "You know your mother?"

"I may have met her, yes." Sarcasm dripped from Linc's voice.

"You both gave blood for Myles's surgery, right?"

"Yes. I have to say, though, she was very reluctant to do it. I thought she might be afraid of needles. Why?"

"There's no easy way to put this—"

"Then just flat out say it, Emilia. Say whatever it is that you clearly don't want to say." Linc's voice rose a whole octave on the last words.

"There's no way your mother is Myles's or your mother."

Linc leapt out of his chair. It clattered to the paving stones that made up his patio. "What the hell are you talking about?"

Chapter 17

Linc could hardly believe the words that came out of Emilia's mouth. His mother was not his mother? It was hard to wrap his head around that idea. He paced on the paving stones and ran his hands through his hair. What craziness was this? He thought back over the years and tried to recall his first cognitive moment. It was no good. With his mind awhirl, Lincoln couldn't focus long enough for that memory to come.

Eventually, he bent and picked up his chair. He sat and shook his head at Emilia. "Thanks for letting me wander about like a lunatic without interrupting me."

She smiled gently. "It seemed that you needed a moment."

"A *moment*? I need an asylum. Do you really believe that my mother may not actually be my mother? How can this be?"

"It can *be*, Linc. It means she didn't give birth to

you. Do you remember any other woman in a parental role at all in your life?"

"I'm trying, but I'm so overwhelmed that I can't focus my thoughts well enough to even recall my first memory. I want to say that Caroline was always there. Always. There was never a question in my mind that the woman was my mother." He made a face. "Of course, there were many times that I wished she wasn't—" He snapped his fingers. "Wait a second. I remembered something."

Emilia leaned forward in her chair. "What?"

"When they came for us to do the blood test in the hospital, Caroline was reluctant like I told you but I wasn't remembering that her husband, the senator, was in the lobby when we came out. When she said to him that she'd given blood, he asked, 'Do you think that was wise,' or something like that."

Emilia nodded. "Sounds to me like he knows the truth."

"What exactly *is* the truth?"

"I'm not an expert on blood typing by any means but here's the gist of it. You and Myles both have type O blood. Caroline has AB. It seems that someone with AB blood can't be the mother of a type O child. So, even without an actual DNA test, she can be excluded as your biological mother."

"This is massive, Emilia. Massive. It explains a lot about the way Myles and I have always been treated by her, but it also opens up a lot of questions, too. Like who was our mother and why is there no trace of her anywhere in that house over on First Street? I sure would like to know the answer to that mystery."

"I'd like some answers too, like why Caroline would even take a chance on giving blood if she thought she might be found out. It seems like an unnecessary risk to me."

"I was giving her a hard time about it. Maybe she did it to get me off her back?" Linc said.

Emilia tapped her right index finger on her chin. "Maybe since she's AB, she thought she could give blood to either A or B people and didn't know you and Myles are O?"

"How could she not know our blood types? That seems unreal to me. Even if she's not our biological mother, she was in our home at least as long as I can remember."

"Have either of you ever had surgery before?"

"No. What does that matter?"

"My mom didn't know my blood type until I was in high school and had to have an emergency appendectomy. They took my type then since I would need blood in the surgery and my folks wanted to donate for me. My surgery wasn't done with a laser since the appendix had already ruptured. It was a full-cut surgery."

"I need to ask Caroline about all this. Since Dad is dead, I can't ask him. His parents died when I was a kid

and so did his brother, so Myles and I are the last Eisenger men. I only have her to ask and I won't even know
if she's lying when she answers me since she seems to be
an expert in not telling the truth." He looked at his watch.
"If it wasn't almost one a.m., I'd call that woman right
now."

"There are other questions, too, that need answers."

"For sure. I want to find out who my mother actually
was. Maybe she still has family—no, chances are if she
did that, they would have come around to see us kids
while we were little. Damn it. I want to know the truth
about all this." He ran his right hand across the top of his
head.

"There's another question you're not thinking about,
Linc, and it's more important than the others." Emilia
reached out and placed her hand on his thigh. "This is
going to be something else hard for you to deal with so
I'm going to say it and then let you think about it overnight. I have to question Mr. Rhodes at the precinct at
nine and we need to get some rest but I want you to think
about this as you go to bed."

"Dear God, what else can there be?"

"After the warden told me and Howard about the
failed blood donation—"

"Ha." Linc's laugh was a short bark. "I like that.
Talk about a euphemism. Geez, Emilia, call it like it is. A
stranger tried to give blood to someone she's not related
to. What's that phrase I'm searching for? Pussyfooting

around? Don't do that. I have more respect for myself than to let you sugar-coat it. I don't need rose-colored glasses, thank you very much."

"Okay fine. You want it rough?" She stood. "How's this for *rough*, Mr. Eisenger? After we got the news about your so-called mother from the warden, Howard and I looked up how your father died. A drowning in their backyard pool? *Really*? Your dad was a champion swimmer in high school and college and he *drowns*? Did you never question that?"

Linc rose and grabbed Emilia's upper arms. "What are you insinuating?"

"I'm not insinuating anything, Linc. I'm asking you flat out to think about *this*. What would this woman— who has a dead husband, one son in prison for murder, and one son who was set up to look like he committed Van Nuys's murder and could easily have gone away for that had we not figured out what the man was really saying with his dying breath—what would she have to gain? In other words, did your dad really drown or was he helped to his death?"

Linc let go of Emilia and staggered backward. Horrified at the implications of what she was saying, he covered his mouth with his hand.

"Think about it, Linc. You haven't gotten out that trust yet. Let's get it now and look at it. Isn't it in your safe?"

"No." Linc shook his head. "It's not here. There's a

copy in my dad's safe at his place and I have another copy in my safe deposit box at the bank. I was planning to get it in the morning. I couldn't get it sooner since we had all that stuff happening at the station. I initially was going to call and see if my banker could meet me over there but it seemed to get later and later and I never did."

"They would've opened the bank for you after hours?"

He shrugged. "Sure."

"Must be nice."

"What?"

"To have that kind of clout."

"Never mind about that. What do you think about the trust being involved in this? I haven't ever really paid attention to the terms of it other than to know that it owns land and administers it for our benefit."

"Here's what I'm thinking—but we need to read the trust to know for sure—a while ago you said in passing that you and Myles are the last Eisenger men. That trust was set up in the 1840s for the benefit of the Eisengers. What happens when there aren't any more?"

"I don't know but how can that matter? There *are* more of us. Myles and I are both alive and still young enough to have children—" Linc stopped short as the light bulb went off.

Emilia nodded. "See where I'm going with this?"

"Wow. I sure do. With Myles in prison convicted of murder and if I was also convicted of a murder, with Dad gone, I bet that Caroline thinks she has a stake in that trust." He sat down hard in his chair and put his head in his hands. "Could she really have arranged for Van Nuys to be killed? In order to try to frame me?"

Emilia knelt beside him and placed her hand on the back of his head. "I think he was killed for two reasons actually."

He didn't look up. "What's the second one?"

"I think she must have asked Van Nuys some questions about the trust. Didn't you say he was a real estate lawyer?"

Linc *did* look up then. "Good God. This really could be it, couldn't it? You may very well have solved this case as well as Myles's case. What are we going to do? How can we trap her into a confession?"

"Don't rush into anything, Linc. We need to move slowly and carefully. I'm still working on the hooker case as well and I probably shouldn't say this but I will. We think they may all be connected."

"How do you figure that? What would either have to do with the other?"

"I can't really discuss that. Let's just say we need to be calm and methodical and be sure we have all the evidence before we strike out, okay?" She smiled. "Now, I have to insist that we go to bed. In the morning, I'll go and question Rhodes and you'll get to the bank and get that trust document. Promise me you won't confront Caroline until we're ready to execute a warrant on her."

"I'll try but I really want to head over there right now and demand answers." Linc stood and ran his hands through his hair again. "And much as I like the invitation to go to bed, I'm sorry we have to go to separate ones."

Emilia grinned. "Me too but you'd be surprised at why."

"Because you think I'm sexy and want to be with me?"

Her smile grew larger. "Besides that."

"What can there be besides that?"

"I want to make sure you don't sneak out and over the three blocks to deal with your former mother."

"I like the sound of former mother but you have to understand that I have no intention of going over there by myself and messing up the case against her. If she did all this to Myles, my dad, Van Nuys, and me, I want her to go down and go down hard."

"You and me both, Mr. Eisenger, you and me both."

∽∾∽

The next morning came all too soon for Emilia. She wagered that she'd slept all of eight hours in the last five days. Her eyes were filled with grit, almost like grains of sand, she was so tired. She didn't even want to look in a mirror as they had to be bloodshot so bad they may have been the same color as a cape that bullfighters use in the ring.

The thought of bullfighters led her brain to rodeos, which led her to Myles. She threw back the covers, along with the plush gray duvet, and made her way to her overnight bag. Time to take a shower and get this case solved. Every day they delayed was another day Myles sat in prison for no reason. Determined to start the wheels of justice in motion, she veered from her bag over to where she'd set her phone to charge. She unhooked it from the charger and dialed Howard's number.

When he picked up, she filled him in quickly on the events of the prior evening and arranged for a guard for Linc as well as a call to the warden to keep Myles away from any visitors. She wasn't taking any chances. After she disconnected the call, she took her bag into the lush en-suite bathroom that was too sinfully elegant to classify as a place to merely prepare for the day ahead. The tub was huge and sunken. It was made of some kind of deep burgundy marble that matched the sheets and pillowcases on the bed that was in the next room. The tub had a lot of jets that Emilia wished she had time to sit and enjoy. Reluctantly, instead, she stepped into the sauna/shower combination and lathered herself.

Stepping out of the luxury, she pulled on her jeans and polo shirt, tousled her still damp hair, and, sliding on her shoes, stepped in to the bedroom. Startled, she jumped a little at the sight of Bobbi, dressed and seated with her feet on the bed.

"Good morning. You look nice," Emilia said. It was

true. The girl wore a bright shirt and long skirt that Emilia had borrowed from Alyce-Faye since the younger girl was actually larger than the detective was.

"Thanks. Linc asked me to come get you. He says breakfast is ready and the bank opens in thirty minutes."

"Ahh, *Mr. I Can Get the Bank Manager to Open at Any Time* wants to dare wait until the bank is actually really open?"

"I don't pretend to understand what you mean by that but I'm starving. Come on." Bobbi stood and grabbed Emilia's hand. "Let's go."

"You seem in good spirits. I'm glad you're not still mad at me for being a cop."

"Linc says he's going to represent me and is going to make sure I'm not sent back to that place."

Emilia didn't want to break the girl's heart but she was afraid that Linc might not be able to pull that off. She decided to let it go for now, besides, it would be better for Linc to take the brunt of the girl's disappointment if he failed than for Emilia herself to be blamed. She knew that was the coward's way out, but so what?

Once they were downstairs and turned the corner toward the kitchen, the aroma of bacon lured Emilia forward. She hadn't realized she was so hungry. "Good morning, Linc."

He glanced up from his work frying eggs. He smiled and it nearly took her breath away. Lord, she wanted a week alone with the man like she'd never wanted time off before. Maybe sometime soon, she could lock herself away with him and see exactly what he was made of. She giggled. He'd never be able to keep up with her once she got her hands on him.

"What's funny?" Linc asked.

Thinking fast, she said, "It's an interesting thing seeing the lawyer, who everyone in town doesn't want to cross-examine them, cooking breakfast, that's all."

Linc raised his eyebrows. He glanced over at Bobbi. "I think there's more to it than that. See how she's blushing?"

"I do." Bobbi laughed. "I'm only fourteen but I think that the detective thinks you're cute, Mr. Eisenger. I know I do but I'm way too young for you."

"Oh, good grief. Hand me some breakfast, Linc. I have to get to the precinct."

"See how she's changing the subject?" Bobbi giggled. "I know I'm right. She likes you."

"Better stop teasing her, Bobbi. I hear she's packing heat." Linc passed a plate of bacon and eggs across the bar to Emilia and then another to Bobbi.

"I'm not yet but I will be before I leave here." Emilia carried her plate to the table, sat down, and dug in. Maybe if she shoveled in food so fast that she couldn't speak, they would leave her alone.

The others joined Emilia at the table. Linc jumped back up in a few seconds. "Sorry. I forgot the toast."

"I'm fine. My ride will be here in a minute."

"Is Howard coming to get you? I thought I would take you and Bobbi over to the precinct."

"Why am I going to the precinct?" Bobbi asked.

"Because I need to make sure you're safe and it may be dangerous right now to be with me on the streets." Linc took a bite of his eggs.

"Speaking of needing to keep safe, this seems like a good time to tell you—" The doorbell rang. Emilia stood. "Let me get that."

"No, wait. I want to hear what it's a good time to tell me about." Linc stood as well and followed her to the door.

She opened it to Howard and a uniformed officer.

"You ready to go, Em?" Howard asked.

"Come in a second. I was finally getting a chance to tell Linc I had a guard coming to be with him on his trip to the bank."

"What? I don't need a guard. What are you talking about?" Linc's expression was one that Emilia was sure had scared many a witness but it didn't frighten her at all. She wanted this man safe and if he got mad at her about it, so what?

Bobbi entered the foyer. "What's this about a guard?"

Great. Now the girl was going to get scared if she heard what was going on. Emilia looked up at Linc. "Is there somewhere in private that we can speak? You and I?"

"The rest of you may as well come on in and eat my food while you wait. There's plenty on the stove. Help yourself." Linc turned to Bobbi. "Will you help them with plates and cups?"

"Sure." Bobbi bounced out of the room with Howard and the uniformed cop on her trail.

"Come with me, Detective."

Linc led Emilia into a small room off the foyer. She took in her surroundings. The room was gorgeous. It was lined on three sides in mahogany wood bookshelves filled with books that actually looked like they'd been read and well-loved. There were two plush wingback chairs with a tall floor lamp between them.

"Wow. What a wonderful room."

Linc shut the door behind them and leaned against it with his arms crossed. "That's not what we're here about. What's this about a guard for me?"

"Whether you like it or not, you're in danger and you need protection. Until we can make our case against Caroline, we need to be sure that you're safe."

"I'm safe. I have a permit to carry a concealed weapon. I have it on in an ankle holster right now. I don't think she'll get the drop on me. I'm alert and ready for them. They won't kill me."

"They could still set you up to go down for something else. That's as scary as them killing you, Linc. Could you stand being arrested and going to prison? Like Myles, it could happen to you. Think of it this way. What if we say that the guard isn't there to protect you—that you can do that for yourself—but that he's there to make sure that we have a witness with you every second, so if they try to pull something to have you arrested, that you'll have someone to say you didn't do anything wrong?"

Linc cracked up. When he regained control, he said, "Have you ever thought about going to law school?"

"No? Why?" She couldn't help herself from smiling at him. His laughter was contagious.

"No, I take that back. You should be a journalist." He nodded. "Yep, that's it. A journalist."

"Why's that?"

"The way you can spin a story is a gift. A rare gift." Linc laughed again and mimicking her higher voice said, "Oh, look, big strong Linc, you can use that gun of yours to protect yourself but let's have you a witness along for the ride in case you need one to cover your butt, but you'll be on your own when it comes to protection."

"So, does this mean you'll do it?"

"Do I really have a choice? I think I'm learning that, when it comes to what Detective Emilia Hammond wants, I have zero ability to say no."

She stepped close to him, into his personal space. "Can you say no to a little kiss before I go?"

"Absolutely not." Linc put his arms around her and lightly placed his lips on hers. He ran his tongue across her bottom lip. She opened her mouth and his tongue found its way inside. For a few moments, she forgot everything and everyone in the world until the knock at the door startled them both.

They leapt apart as if they were two students caught smoking in the lavatory by the meanest dean on campus.

"Come on, Em. We're going to be late. Rhodes is coming in for questioning today."

"On the way, Howard." Emilia smiled at Linc. "When this is over and I mean when Myles is out of prison, because only then will it truly be over, I want to spend a solid week here with you. No interruptions, no work, no partners, and no cases, okay?"

Linc winked. "You won't get any arguments from me."

"Hmm. A lawyer not making arguments. I think I could handle that."

"You won't be able to handle *me*, Detective. I'm going to give you a work out you won't soon forget." Linc opened the door.

"Promises, promises." Emilia grinned and stepped out in front of Linc.

"What's he promising?" Howard asked.

"To do whatever his protection officer says."

"Somehow I doubt that, Em. I really do." Howard laughed and they all headed out to the cars in the driveway.

Chapter 18

The interrogation of Michael Rhodes went smoothly, if a little off course. He was cocky and self-assured like he'd been at the rodeo. After a lot of dancing around the subject, he finally admitted to being in the French Quarter both at the time the first young prostitute was killed and, then again, when the second one was beaten. He denied any involvement in the crimes, and wouldn't tell why he was hanging around the Quarter, but confessed to seeing someone following the girl who was beaten. He wasn't sure about the other girl as he said he didn't recognize her picture.

Emilia wasn't sure he was telling the truth about not knowing who she was from the picture taken by the coroner. Those photos were always a little off-putting and people really didn't appear the same dead as they did alive. The spark of life that made them who they were—their personality so to speak—disappeared from the face, and sometimes it was hard to identify someone who may not have been well-known to the witness. She thought she'd seen a glimmer of recognition in Rhodes's eyes as he glanced at the picture. How convenient for him as well, if he only admitted to recognizing the one who was still alive. If he was worried about charges against him, an assault and battery charge was better than a murder one any day.

Emilia told him not to go out of state and to stay available in case they needed him to testify. She then cut him loose. That's when things got a little weird.

Rhodes stepped out of the interrogation room with Emilia right behind him and he almost ran straight into Bobbi.

Bobbi gasped and stepped back with a horrified expression on her face. She was so pale, Emilia dashed around Rhodes and grabbed the girl's arm.

"What's wrong, Bobbi?"

"Roberta Jones. Do you have any idea how hard I've been looking for you? Where have you been? Your father is frantic to get you home. I've been all over this city trying to find you and here you are in the police station. What kind of luck is that?" Rhodes took a step toward Bobbi.

Bobbi backed away with a wild look in her eyes. "What have you done, Emilia? I thought you and Linc were going to help me. You called Rhodes to come get me, didn't you? How could you?"

"I don't have a clue what you're talking about, Bobbi. I didn't know you even knew Michael Rhodes. He's a witness in one of my cases. I'd been planning to talk to him this morning before I ever even met you."

"I don't believe you. How could you betray me? I thought you were my friend." Bobbi appeared to be about to bolt out of the station so Emilia reached out for her. "Get your hands off me," Bobbi screamed.

The captain stepped out of his office. "What's all the ruckus out here?"

"I've got this under control, Captain."

"Clearly you don't, Detective Hammond, since there's a disturbance in my stationhouse. All of you, come with me into this interrogation room."

The captain strode across the space and into the doorway leading to the room Emilia and Rhodes had vacated.

Bobbi shook her head. "I'm not going in there with him." She pointed at Rhodes. "No way."

"In my precinct house, young woman, everyone does what I say. You will come in here and you'll do it now."

"Come on. I won't let anything happen to you," Emilia said.

The girl crossed her arms and sulked. "Like I trust you now."

"Whether you believe me or not is not important. I'm going to help you. Now come on before the captain gets mad. That's not a pretty sight."

Emilia entered the room, pulling Bobbi along with her.

Rhodes followed them.

When they were all seated, the captain turned to Rhodes. "Explain how you know this girl."

"I know her father. We met through the livestock business. When Roberta ran away, he learned from one of her friends that she was headed to New Orleans. He knew I was in the area for the Angola October rodeos with my bulls and asked me to see if I could find her and get her home. That was the real reason I was trolling the red light district. The reason I didn't tell you earlier. I was searching for my friend's daughter."

The captain faced Bobbi. "Is this true? Do you know this man to be a friend of your father's?"

Bobbi crossed her arms over her chest. "I know him and I know that the man he calls my father knows him."

The captain frowned at the girl. "So why shouldn't I call child care services and have them release you into his custody so he can take you home?"

Bobbi burst into tears and clutched Emilia's arm so hard Emilia knew she was going to leave a nasty bruise. "Call my lawyer. You can't let him do this. Call Mr. Eisenger."

"You have a lawyer?"

Rhodes asked the question in a tone of voice that alerted Emilia that something was amiss—something besides a young girl trying to avoid being sent home to an environment that she was merely displeased with. Something wasn't kosher in Minnesota.

"What's the deal, Bobbi? Why are you terrified?" As she spoke, it became clear to Emilia that the girl really was absolutely paralyzed with fear. "Tell me and the captain why this man scares you like this."

"He's lying about my father."

"You said not more than a minute ago that he knows your father." The captain was losing patience, Emilia could tell.

"I think she said that he knows the man who calls himself her father. That seems like a technical difference, Captain." Emilia patted Bobbi's shoulder. "Tell us exactly what you meant by what you said."

"Make him leave first. He'll say I'm lying and you'll believe him because he's a grown-up and I'm not. I may be young but I know how this works. Kids get ignored all the time. I've tried to tell the truth before and no one believes me."

"I'm losing my patience with you, young lady, and I want you to answer me right now or I'll shut this conversation down all the way and no one will talk to you until the authorities show up and take you back to Minnesota. I'm not kidding around and I'm not asking Mr. Rhodes to leave. You either tell us all or you tell no one," the captain said.

Emilia could hardly believe how harsh the captain was being with a little girl. He usually was much nicer.

She wanted to interfere but knew she couldn't or he would write her up for insubordination.

"All right then." Bobbi huffed out a deep breath and making eye contact with only Emilia, she added, "The man who says he is my father, isn't. He *bought* me from my strung-out doped-up mother when she was down on her luck. He took us in initially and said he was going to help her get on her feet but what he actually did was continue to provide her with needles and the junk to shoot up with."

Michael Rhodes let out a small noise.

The captain held up his hand to silence the man and nodded his encouragement to Bobbi to go on with her story.

She continued without glancing in Rhodes's direction. "When my mother was on her death bed, she asked the man to promise to take care of me. She had no idea he'd been raping me since we'd been in his house. I tried to tell her but she was only interested in the next high."

Bobbi wiped an errant tear off her face. Emilia wasn't sure if she was crying for her lost mother or for herself. Watching her was heart-wrenching.

"Do you believing this crap?" Rhodes asked.

"Shush. Let the girl finish," the captain said.

"Anyway, while she was dying, he had a lawyer come in with some documents and two witnesses. The agreement was that he would pay for her funeral and a headstone and that, in exchange, she would let him adopt me. I was adopted by a pedophile rapist and there was no way to get free. I tried. I really tried, Emilia, but they always brought me back. I thought this time would be different." Bobbi collapsed in Emilia's arms and wailed. "I can't go back. I'll kill myself before I go back to Minnesota."

Emilia patted the girl to soothe her. "Hang on a minute, Bobbi. We're going to find out about this. If you were adopted, there will be records of it, and if this man is hurting you, you shouldn't have to go back."

"You aren't serious. You can't believe what she's saying. We all know she's a little liar. Her father is devastated that she's gone and he has a right to have her returned to him." Rhodes puffed out his chest as if he were someone important.

"Regardless, Mr. Rhodes, the NOPD will be checking out her story before we let her leave." The captain stood and placed his hands flat on the table as he addressed Bobbi. "I'm going to see what I can find out and I hope you aren't playing me."

Bobbi scrubbed her face with the heels of her hands. "I'm not."

"You know you can't get adoption records, right? They're sealed, aren't they? And besides, how are you going to get something that doesn't exist in the first place?" Rhodes now seemed to be the one who was pouting.

Emilia stood as well. "I'm taking her to the break

room while you see what's up, Captain. Is that all right?"

"Yeah, and, Mr. Rhodes?" The captain turned to the man. "You can leave your phone number with the desk clerk and when we know if we're releasing this girl to you, we'll call you."

Bobbi's eyes widened but before she could react and cry some more, Emilia pulled her out of the interrogation room.

Once they were out of the hearing of the captain and Rhodes, Emilia said, "I'm calling Linc. Right now. Come on." She led the girl down the hallway to the private area for the staff.

၈၁၈၁

Linc's phone rang as he was leaving the bank with the trust documents. He glanced down at the caller ID. It was Caroline. He let the call go to voicemail. He wasn't ready to speak with her yet. She was going to be dealt with but he wanted to be sure that he didn't blow the case by talking to her unprepared. He knew she'd probably call again as that was her pattern but he was *not* going to answer.

He hadn't remembered that the trust documents were so voluminous. He'd spent a few minutes in the room where the customers were led to review items in their safe deposit boxes thinking he could find what he needed quickly. After scanning the document for a bit, he finally decided that he needed to get the whole thing to Emilia and Howard and let them take a look so they could plan the next step. He was determined to figure out if this woman who he'd thought his whole life was his mother was actually behind all the death and devastation that had hit the Eisenger family in the last couple of years.

That thought stopped him short. If Caroline had been married to his father all that time, why now? Why did she suddenly, a couple of years ago, decide that she needed to take the actions she'd taken? It was a mind-numbing thought.

There had to be an impetus for her to do what she did. Was it meeting the senatorial candidate? The now-senator and husband of the woman? The person who used his father's money to pay for his campaign?

He followed the uniformed patrolman out of the bank and to his car. "Thanks for coming with me. I told Emilia that it wouldn't be necessary but she's pretty stubborn."

"You got that right. All of us at the precinct think she's a kick-butt officer but, man, she's one hard-headed chick."

"Does she have a steady guy?" Linc wasn't sure he wanted the man to know he was interested in Emilia but he had to know if there was anyone else in her life. She'd been more than open to his kisses but he was still compelled to ask.

"No. She doesn't. I think any man who wants to see

her on a personal basis is going to have a tough road ahead of him."

Linc clicked the button on his car key to unlock the doors. "Why's that?"

"She's married to the job. Emilia has *got* to be the most focused girl I have ever met. She made detective faster than anyone in the history of the NOPD." The officer opened the door and they got in. Once Linc cranked the engine, he added, "So if you're interested in the girl, your competition is her gold shield. Good luck to you."

Linc grinned. "I think I can handle that. I've been kind of married to my own job for too long. Maybe we can both separate a little—not totally divorce our jobs— just separate from them once in a while."

"Hats off to you then. I hope you land her. She's a great chick."

"Let's go see her and her partner so we can resolve this case of mine and then maybe I can sweep her off her feet." Linc drove out of the bank's parking lot.

"Sounds good to me."

They'd gone five blocks when Linc's phone rang. He clicked the Bluetooth button on his steering wheel to answer the phone. He might have held the phone to his ear but he remembered there was a cop in the car with him and, in case the guy wanted to arrest him for chatting on the phone in the car, he answered with the Bluetooth.

Feeling cocky, he said, "Hello."

"Linc? It's Emilia."

"Yeah, it's me. We're on our way to the precinct. What's up?"

"Some interesting developments related to Bobbi. Right now, she's in a jam and we need you to get here soon. I was checking in to make sure you were headed here instead of studying the documents. We still need to do that but, right now, this Bobbi thing has hit the fan."

"Without speeding, we'll be there in less than ten minutes. How's that?"

"Good. Hurry."

"Can you tell me what's going on so I can be ready?"

"I'll fill you in when you get here. She's not hurt but she needs a lawyer."

"Geez. Everything you say is making me more anxious, not less. She hasn't been arrested has she?"

"No but the captain is making noises about sending her to Minnesota today."

"I'm on my way. The heck with not speeding." Linc disconnected the call and glanced over at his guard. "Sorry, man, gotta go."

His passenger laughed. "I won't tell. I only wish I had a portable siren. We'd turn that puppy on."

Linc pressed the accelerator and barreled down the road until they got close to the tourist area and he had to slow to a crawl. They made it to the precinct parking area and Linc was almost out of the Lexus before he put it in park.

He grabbed the papers he'd retrieved from the bank,

darted into the building, and up the stairs, taking them two at a time. When he arrived at the bullpen area leading to the detective's desks, Howard glanced up from his workstation and called out, "Em, Mr. Eisenger is here."

Linc stepped closer to the bullpen but was almost knocked over before he could get near Howard. Bobbi had thrown herself at him and stood sobbing into his chest.

"What is this all about?" Linc asked Emilia who was directly behind them.

"Come into the interrogation room and we'll tell you all about it," Emilia said.

"I think I should meet with Bobbi alone. Some of the things she may want to say to me may be privileged. Sorry."

"No, you're right. It's fine."

Linc was sure it probably wasn't fine. He could tell from the tone of Emilia's voice that she was ticked off. Too bad. He had to do his job.

As a kind of peace offering, he held out the trust documents. "In case you're bored while I'm chatting with my client, here's some interesting reading material for you two."

Emilia reached for them. "Thanks. We'll be reviewing these for evidence of motive. I'm pretty curious about what's in them that would be worth taking several lives for."

"I'm curious, too, Em. Bring them over here," Howard said.

Emilia pointed to the interrogation room. "You and Bobbi can go in there and talk. I hope you have a productive meeting."

"And I hope you and Howard do as well."

Linc smiled. He wanted to let her know he didn't want to leave her out of the conversation with Bobbi and that he wouldn't, except that the girl was his client and obviously needed him and his expertise. This meeting needed to be out of the hearing and knowledge of law enforcement, especially since the captain himself might be the one who Linc needed to take action against to protect his client. Since the captain was Emilia's boss, she could very well end up in an awkward position. He didn't want that for her.

Chapter 19

Emilia found the operative paragraph buried fifteen pages back in the trust documents. Otto Eisenger established the trust in 1849 when he was in his early thirties. His wife was expecting their first child and Otto had been purchasing parcels of land around the city, as well as on the shores of Lake Pontchartrain. He also was buying up properties that had been underwater in the flood of May 1849 that started at the plantation of Pierre Sauvé and ran down into the city from the Mississippi River. A large number of the owners of those flooded properties sold out in order not to incur the expenses of rehabilitation and repairs from the waters that ruined their properties.

Otto purchased several parcels in the lower Garden District as well as the central business district. He decided to have a trust drawn to protect the interests of his heirs. Over the years, as Emilia and Howard could tell, by the listing of properties held by the trust, the amount of wealth represented by these properties grew to huge proportions. The city changed over the years and some of the residential parcels Otto bought were now bars, inns, and other commercial buildings, as well as a few skyscraper office complexes. The trust drew income from them all.

The most important paragraph of the initial trust, which had been repeated in all updates to the documents, stated that when the last of the Eisenger heirs passed away that the trust corpus would vest in a number of charities and any surviving spouses. Emilia gasped when she read those words. "Who would do such a thing? It seems a bit weird, doesn't it?"

"To us as cops, yes. It gives a motive for murder to any one of the Eisenger wives or husbands over the years. Of course, since this wasn't well known, there wouldn't be anything for the Eisenger bloodline to worry about until it was public knowledge. As it is, it's buried pretty deep in a bunch of legalese."

"And it also may not have meant much in the early days since the properties have really only gotten more and more valuable as the centuries have gone on. I mean, when Otto was buying them, they would've been more expensive to repair and maintain than they would've had money coming in on them. If these trusts have been locked in safes for years, chances of a spouse knowing that the terms were these would be slim."

"I wonder when Linc's mother found out about it. If

she's the one behind all these crimes like we think she is, she had to learn about it sometime before Linc's dad died and Myles was arrested." Howard flipped some pages. "Who administers this trust? Can you tell from these?"

"My bank. It's always been handled by the bank. Dad said that no one ever changed it since it would be such a hassle for an individual to handle all the properties and the rents involved, to say nothing of the repairs and maintenance." Linc walked over from the interrogation room. He smiled at Bobbi and handed her his phone. "Hang out over there for a bit. You can play some games on my phone. Download whatever you want."

"Thanks." The smile Bobbi gave him as she left to sit on the bench along the wall was the first Emilia had seen from the girl that made her actually look her age.

"What did you find?" Linc pulled up a chair.

Emilia told him about the provision regarding the last Eisenger. As she talked, she could see his expression change from confusion to certainty. When she was finished with the explanation, she asked, "When do you think Caroline knew about the way the trust ends?"

Linc scowled. "I know exactly when she found out."

"You *do*?"

"Well, not really the exact moment but I do know when she *wanted* to know. I can trace it back to about six months before Dad died."

"What happened?" Howard asked.

"We were all at dinner at Brennan's. Myles and I

were telling Dad about the charitable foundation we wanted to set up to care for the girls and boys on the streets who, for whatever reason, couldn't return to their homes and who really weren't being properly cared for by social services. Dad was talking about the trust and how he'd have to go to the trustees at the bank to see if we could convert the use of one of the properties for this purpose."

"And Caroline was there as well?" Emilia asked.

"Yeah." Linc nodded. "Caroline was there and full of questions about the trust and why my dad couldn't merely tell the bankers that we needed the property and make them deed it over to us. Dad tried to explain to her about the number of family members who have benefited over the years from the trust. He explained that he didn't have the authority to invade the principal of the trust—he only had the right to the income from it."

Emilia flipped the page on the pad where she'd been making some notes. "And what did she do?"

"She insisted that he show her the documents and he promised to get his copy out of the safe at the house and let her look at it when they got home." Linc shook his head as if he were sad. "And to think, Myles and I thought she was actually upset that Dad couldn't give us the land and building we wanted to use for our facility. We couldn't believe she was finally getting behind us on a project. I guess we should've known better."

"Do you know if you father ever showed her?" Emilia asked.

"I haven't got a clue but I assume that she found out somehow because, if not, we have no suspect, do we?"

"True, but what I'm asking is if you know if *he* showed her?"

"Why does that matter?"

"Linc, I think we need to find out for sure if your father died of drowning or had some help. We—" Emilia pointed from herself to Howard. "—want to go to the courts and have him exhumed."

"Don't look at her like that, Linc, it was my idea." Howard tapped the tabletop. "We know she was technically the next of kin when he died. But if we can pin the murder of Van Nuys on her and tie it to the Eisenger trust, then you and Myles will be the ones who have the right to consent to the exhumation, because we'll have probable cause against her and she won't be able to stop us. Promise you'll think about it. It's premature as yet but, if this woman killed your father, don't you want her to go down for that as well as all the other things we think she did?"

"Yeah, I do but it's hard to take that in right now. Let's plan how we're going to get Caroline for Clifford Van Nuys and get Myles out of prison. We can worry about Dad later, okay?"

Howard rubbed his hands together. "All right then. What's the plan?"

"I want to confront her. Can I wear a wire and go over to the house that she still lives in? The one where Dad died and then she moved in that senator."

"I'm not sure that's a good idea, Linc. If she were setting you up to take the fall for either Van Nuys's death or the young prostitute's, you would be at her mercy. It seems to me that she has Myles out of the way where he can't reproduce and have another Eisenger who would be a beneficiary of the trust. He was also injured at the rodeo and she may have somehow arranged that to get him out of the way altogether. She could shoot you or kill you some other way and make it appear as if you attacked her and she had to defend herself." Emilia repressed a shudder at the thought of Linc dying.

"First of all, she very well could have arranged that issue with the saddle as she and Senator Phelps were there and he actually said something along the lines of having taken care of some issue." Linc ran his hand over his face before continuing. "Secondly, if I wear a wire, she can't set me up at all. You'll all be on the other end monitoring the conversation."

"Things can still go wrong, Linc. I'd rather try it another way before we do that. Let's call her in and interrogate her," Emilia said.

"She's too slick for that. You'll never break her. I can do it. I know I can. Let me try."

"How about we lay a little groundwork first?" Howard asked.

"In what way? She called me earlier this morning when I was in the bank. We hardly ever talk but I can call her back now and arrange to visit her. It would seem very natural since she already made contact today. She would be very suspicious if I called her out of the blue since I never do that so now is better than later."

"I think we need to talk to Myles first. He doesn't know we suspect Caroline and he may have some insight about all this. I also think we need to show him the picture of the prostitute who was killed. Maybe he knew her."

"What makes you think that, Howard?" Emilia asked.

"Here's my theory since I heard what Linc said a moment ago. I think that Caroline found out about the last surviving Eisenger provision and made her plans to be that widow left standing at the end. She somehow arranged for Linc's father, Oliver, to die and then she focused on the sons. She set Myles up to take the fall for that clerk's death. She had to have some kind of assistance—we know Simon Bolger testified about the gun being bought by Myles. The question becomes, how did a Garden District sheltered woman find Simon Bolger?"

"We know she wasn't born in the Garden District," Linc said.

"Exactly." Howard nodded. "Let's take this a step further. She talks to a prostitute on the streets and asks for a hook-up for a firearm. Maybe she says she can't go to the store and get one as there will be a check of her background. So maybe she tells this hooker some story about having been in the life herself and trying to keep that a secret and that if the cops run her record, she won't get the gun and her husband will learn the truth about her. Never mind that she's a widow now. She wouldn't tell the girl that part."

Getting into the spirit of the thing, Emilia said, "And when she got what she wanted and Myles was convicted, she had to take care of the witness and had the hooker killed."

"How would Van Nuys fit in and why didn't Caroline kill Bolger?" Linc asked. "As long as you are making stuff up, you may as well take care of those people, too."

"This is how cases are solved. Brainstorming and tossing ideas around," Emilia said.

Linc stood. "I would prefer to solve it by action, not talk. I'm taking Bobbi back to my house and then I'm going to have a chat with Caroline Phelps. You two suit yourselves but I'm gone." He stalked over to Bobbi, said something to her in a whisper, and they turned and walked out into the hallway leading to the staircase.

಩಩

Outside, Linc and Bobbi headed to his Lexus. He opened the passenger door for her. She slid in and he leaned on the window frame to speak to her.

"I'm going to do something that may be foolish and dangerous and, before I do, I'm going to call a friend so that if I die doing what I need to do, you'll be taken care of. I promise you that you won't have to go back to Minnesota and that monster, no matter what happens. Do you trust me?"

"I do but I can't let you go do what you said you were going to. I heard you all talking, and I may be a kid, but even I know this woman Caroline is capable of killing you without thinking twice about it. I think you should do like the detectives asked. Go in slower so you're sure to be safe. I'm not being selfish saying that. I really like you and that Emilia, too. I don't want you to get hurt."

"You may be a kid by age but you aren't by experience, Bobbi. Please understand that I need to get this done and behind me. I want my brother home and out of that prison." Linc shut the door and walked around to his own side of the car.

When he was in the car and backing out of the parking space, Bobbi reached over to touch him on the wrist. "Let me go with you. Don't drop me off at your house. Take me to Caroline's with you."

He glanced over at her and then into the rearview mirror. "In the last few moments, you acknowledged that what I was planning to do is dangerous for me. What makes you think it wouldn't be for you, too? Can't you see that I can't take you into that environment? The woman has probably already killed or arranged to kill three other people as well as beat another one up. What makes you think you'd be safe?"

"Can't you see that it doesn't matter if I'm not safe?"

Linc pulled back into the parking space he'd vacated and put the car in park. He turned to face her full on. "It *does* matter. You've been through so much in your life and you deserve a chance at happiness. I want you to have that, so yes, it *does* matter."

"What I mean is that I can't be sitting at your house eating potato chips and kicking back while you're in a place where you can be hurt or killed. I could help. I'd at least be a witness for you if Caroline tried to hurt you."

In a bit of a panic at her words, Linc decided he needed to ask the girl what she thought their relationship was. She sounded like she thought they were a couple. He wanted to set her straight on that but how to do it without hurting her feelings?

She saved him the trouble. "Linc, you're looking at me as if you think you're going to break my heart. You aren't. I get it. You're at least thirty and I'm only fourteen. Don't worry. I'm not transferring hero worship into love. If I was older, yeah, maybe I'd have the hots for you but, really, I'm grateful that you're rescuing me and I want to return the favor. I want to help and I actually think I can. I think this Caroline woman would be less likely to feel threatened if you had a kid with you when you confront her."

"You might be right but I can't take you. You're a

minor and I'm already on thin ice with the state agency in trying to keep you here. We're going to have a hearing with the judge soon and I don't want there to be question that this is the place for you to stay. Can't you see that the risk to you is not only the fact that Caroline is probably a homicidal maniac but that the state will say I'm not fit to keep you?"

"You're going to keep me?" Bobbi tilted her head. "What do you mean? I thought I'd be going to foster care."

"You will, but I plan to get qualified and take you myself if I can."

She burst out laughing.

"What?"

"Do you really think that the state—any state— would let a single man be the foster father of a teenage girl?"

He grinned. "They will here."

"And why is that? Why are you so sure about that?"

"I'm an Eisenger and we get what we want—most of the time, anyway." Linc hoped he was telling her the truth. He'd always believed that he couldn't be hurt by his city or his state but that was before the whole thing happened with Myles and the murder charge.

"I hope you're right and, if you are, what can it hurt to take me with you to Caroline's? If Eisengers are lucky, then we'll pull this off with no problem."

Linc turned to face the steering wheel. He restarted

the car. "Good try but no way am I going to say yes. Let's get you to my house and find that bag of potato chips."

Chapter 20

Frustrated and a bit frightened that Linc had gone rogue, Emilia paced the floor at the precinct. He hadn't even waited for them to discuss anything or to get a warrant or even try to reason with him over the use of a wire. She knew she was becoming more agitated by the moment as Howard discussed the plan of action with the captain. She couldn't very well run after Linc without getting in trouble herself.

Hoping that having Bobbi in the car with him would make Linc stop and think about what he was doing before heading over to Caroline's house, Emilia waited impatiently for the go-ahead from the captain.

After what seemed like a year but was more like fifteen minutes, the captain gave his permission for them to drive by the house on First Street where Caroline lived. He didn't allow them to interfere or enter the premises unless there was a clear and present danger. If they saw anyone breaking the law or in danger, they could go in. In the meantime, he was going to take the paperwork to the courthouse himself to see if he could convince a judge to give them a warrant on what information they had on hand.

Emilia wasn't sure the captain could convince a judge that they were on the right track because of the way New Orleans politics worked and had always worked. The wealthy or prominent citizens seemed to be given a lot of deference and respect. It took a lot to arrest them or to even search for evidence to do so. She sure hoped the captain had on his persuasive pants today.

As the two of them drove from the precinct toward St. Charles Avenue, Howard glanced over toward Emilia several times. He was annoying her immensely.

She finally asked, *"What?"*

"You got it bad for this Eisenger guy, don't you?"

Emilia crossed her arms. "I have no idea what you're talking about."

"I've known you for a long time, missy, and I can tell you're smitten with the man. I have to warn you, though, chances of a biracial gal from Algiers and a wealthy white boy from the Garden District making a go of it are pretty slim—especially when the gal is a little slip of a thing with an uncommonly sassy tongue. You know I love you but you are *not* the country club, tennis playing type."

"First, you're all wrong about Linc and me but, second, you also know me well enough to know that if I wanted that man—I'm saying *if*—I would have him and I'd do my level best to be the kind of woman he would be proud to have on his arm." Emilia adjusted her hips on the car seat so that she could partially face Howard. "Besides, I'm descended from one of the free men of color of this city and my family has been here longer than those Eisenger upstarts. We got here way back in the 1700s."

"Don't go getting all defensive on me, Em. I'm merely making an observation."

"You can stop it any time then." She looked out the window. No way was she going to tell Howard about the kisses she'd shared with Linc Eisenger. He'd have a regular old field day with that information. She recognized the area they were driving through. They were nearing their destination and had one more turn to make.

"You know if you wanted to give it a go with him, I'd wish you the best, right?"

"Sounds like you already decided the whole thing would be doomed before it started."

Could Howard be right? Should she forget those spectacular kisses and move on before she got hurt? He was right about one thing, for sure, she'd never fit in with the hoity-toity Mardi Gras Krewe, debutante, Saints season ticket holder crowd. Was it worth getting her teeth kicked in by some barracuda with family traceable back to Napoleon?

Even if she and Linc could make it work, would she

be accepted by the people he surrounded himself with?

"Maybe not. I know how determined you can be and it seems to me that Lincoln Eisenger is different from the normal Garden District snobs we all know. Ignore me and go for it if that's what you want."

"Thanks for your permission." Emilia's voice dripped with sarcasm. "Look, here's the address. Pull up past it a few houses so we can watch without being noticed."

"I see Linc's car parked across the street. I wonder why he didn't park in the driveway."

"I don't know but he, for sure, has to be already in there since his car is empty. He must have dropped Bobbi off fast and kept driving since we were close behind him."

"We weren't close. It took a while to convince the captain to let us come. You paced a hole in the linoleum waiting for him to set us loose. Did you already forget that?"

"Yeah. I guess I did. Linc has had plenty of time to get inside and get himself killed." Her gut plummeted as she said the words. What if he really did go in there and die?

"What ho, look at that," Howard said.

"What?" Emilia tossed her head and stretched to look over the seatback to see what Howard meant.

"There goes our little Bobbi. She must have decided to follow Linc from his house a few blocks from here, as

I'm sure he wouldn't risk bringing her with him. Way too dangerous for her." Howard pointed and Emilia saw the girl skulking in the bushes outside the house.

"What do you think, Howard? Is this probable cause? Can we follow her since she's a minor?"

"You know we can't."

Bobbi kept moving and was on the porch in a few seconds.

"What about if she opens the door? Wouldn't that be breaking and entering?"

"You really want to arrest that girl after all she's been through, Em?"

"Of course not. I want to protect Linc from a homicidal, lying cow and I'm trying to think of any way at all that I can do that."

"You *are* in love. I can tell. Stop denying it but also stop trying to use Bobbi to get in there. Any excuse we use to get in, believe me, that woman will use at her trial as a defense and we don't want to be forced to arrest the girl."

"Okay, now I know why you're the senior detective."

"Why? Because I ferreted out that you're in love with the white boy?"

"No, because you are more level-headed than me in a crisis."

"You'll learn. All it takes is experience." Howard laughed. "And don't think I didn't notice that this time you didn't bother to deny your feelings for Linc."

Before Emilia could respond, gunshots rang out.

She flung her car door open and, in the same moment, yelled, "Call it in, call it in."

Jerking her service weapon out of her shoulder holster, she ran toward the house.

∾∾∾

As soon as Caroline invited him in, Linc knew he had to hide the fact that he now knew he faced his and Myles's worst enemy. What this woman had done to his family was shameful and unpardonable, but he swallowed his distaste in the name of getting to the truth about what really happened to shatter their happy life. He was curious as well about the cover up for their entire lives that she wasn't their mother. He decided to lead with that information.

Caroline led Linc through the three-story-high foyer. He glanced up at the massive chandelier his father had always told him and Myles that his great grandfather Franklin brought back from his honeymoon in Paris as a gift for his own father, James. The house had been in the family since 1882. Yet another thing this woman had stolen from his family. Yeah, the house had been put into the trust in a later version to protect it from any future heir's financial foibles so it still technically was Eisenger property but this woman was living in it with her new husband and, on top of everything else, that sat wrong with Linc.

When they walked through the formal living room that Caroline had redecorated in some kind of large cabbage rose pink and white upholstered pieces, Linc was a little apprehensive about what she may have done to his father's study, which was where, he realized, she was leading him. He was relieved when they turned the corner near the back of the house. The den still had the same plush leather sofas and dark wood tables that his dad had chosen when the room had to be refurbished after storm damage had marred some of the items.

"Come and sit." Caroline pointed at one of the chairs. She looked immaculate as always, dressed in a black suit and pumps. "I've asked Clara to bring tea. I'm sure you remember her. She's still here, even though all the others who worked here when Oliver was alive are gone."

"I don't need any tea."

"Why are you so grumpy? I thought it was nice of you to call to ask to see me. I didn't think it was because something was wrong."

"You called me first, didn't you? Something about the warden not letting you see Myles. Did you find out why?" Linc hadn't sat and noticed that Caroline hadn't either but that she was starting to appear apprehensive.

Deciding to stay standing to keep her off balance, Linc smiled inwardly. Yes, his law school training was going to help him here. It was all about strategy.

"No, sadly I didn't get through to the warden. I have no clue why they wouldn't let me see Myles. The senator and I drove all the way back up there to visit him and they wouldn't let me in."

"I think I can answer that riddle for you. I've got a few questions about it myself that I hope you'll answer for me after I answer yours."

"Please sit." Caroline nodded at the chair.

"No, I don't think so. This isn't going to be a pleasant conversation and I don't really want to get comfortable."

"What are you carrying on about? Sit and tell me what you think you know about the warden and why you seem to be out of sorts. I haven't seen you in this kind of snit since you and that Belafonte boy got in that fight over that girl in the eleventh grade."

Linc decided to come right out and tell her the news. "Remember when we gave blood for Myles' surgery?"

"I think so, Linc. I'm not senile, you know. It *was* only a few days ago." She sounded cool and collected but Linc could see some redness creeping up from her chest to her neck.

"Imagine my surprise when I found out the truth, *Caroline*." He emphasized her first name so she'd realize that he knew she wasn't his mother. "So, tell me, how did you pull this off for so many years? Why did you and my father think it was so important to lie to my brother and me and, most importantly, who *was* my mother?"

Caroline flopped into the nearest chair. He'd never seen her sit without perfect posture. It actually startled him a bit when she put her head in her hands. Linc noticed she was careful not to muss her hair, though. "I'm sorry. We never wanted you two to know about your mother. We married when you were almost three and Myles was about nine months old."

"Look me in the eye and tell me what happened to my mother and who she was."

"Your mother was a beautiful socialite from Baton Rouge named Samantha Brooks."

"What happened to her and, if she was a socialite, what about her parents or siblings? Surely, they would've wanted to see their grandsons or nephews. You can't tell me they *all* disappeared. What about people of this city? Somebody in this town had to know this woman was married to my father and had two children with him. This is crazy. I don't believe you."

"She got post-partum depression after your brother was born. She killed herself, Linc. Myles was tiny and I was the nanny. I found her body. She hung herself and I found her." Caroline buried her face in her hands again. She sobbed.

Linc didn't believe her but he figured his dad probably fell for her act. She probably laid on the tears and made herself indispensable to the widower with two small children. It still didn't answer what happened to his mother's family though. He pressed on. "What about Samantha Brooks's family? Why didn't they visit us?"

Caroline made eye contact with Linc. Her face was impassive and there were no tear tracks. "At first they did. They were around a lot but they eventually stopped calling and coming by. I think they blamed your father for not getting her the help she needed and it got easier to stay away. You know how some people are. They're all about appearances and really aren't capable of showing love. I tell you, I see it all the time in the upper classes."

Linc snorted then clapped his hands. "Bravo, Caroline. You're something else."

"What?" She seemed truly befuddled.

"You are the very person you describe. I understand it more now—the amount of parental affection Myles and I received from you was virtually nil but I get it now—you didn't care because you weren't our mother. *You* are one of those people who only care about appearances."

"Well, now that you know, I guess you'll be telling Myles and we won't be seeing either of you again."

"I have a few more things I want to address before I go."

"You do know that, as your father's widow, I have the right to stay in this house as long as I live, right?"

"Sadly, I don't think Dad intended you to live with another man in his bedroom."

"Too bad. That's the way his will was written and the trust as well."

"And that brings me to my next questions." Linc crossed his arms and eyed the distance to the door. If she tried to pull anything, he wanted to know how far he was to getting out, either back through to the foyer or to the exit out the side door to the *porte cochere*.

"What questions?"

"What did you find out about the family trust? And more importantly, *when* did you find out?"

"I don't know what you mean." Caroline stood and edged toward the desk over by the window.

"Sure you do. Remember that dinner at Brennan's a few months before Dad died? What did you learn that made you go off the rails?" Linc knew he was getting ahead of himself but the smug expression on her face was making him lose perspective.

"What do you mean by that? What off the rails? I've done nothing." She moved a bit closer to the desk.

"Don't move one more inch." Linc pointed at the large partner's desk. "Don't think I don't remember that Dad kept his gun in the top row of that desk. The mere fact that you're trying to get there shows me that you know you've been caught. We know what you've done. There's no more hiding, Caroline."

"You don't know anything you stupid boy." At the same time Caroline lunged for the desk, the senator entered the room with a pistol in his hand. He pointed it straight at Linc's heart.

In that split-second, Linc knew he was dead. His

fleeting thought was that he hoped Emilia would keep trying to get Myles freed from prison.

At the moment Linc realized the senator was pulling the trigger, Bobbi ran in the room and shoved Phelps at the same time she yelled, "Watch out, Linc."

The sound of the gun going off reverberated in the room but the shot went wild with the bullet smashing into the ceiling. Debris fell to the carpeting.

Bobbi landed on top of the senator when he fell on the floor.

Linc ducked down and flipped the coffee table up on its side. He peered over at Bobbi where she was wrestling with Phelps. His heart in his throat, he couldn't make a sound but, determined to assist the girl, he tried to work his way over to them.

Another shot rang out. More of the ceiling fell. Linc glanced up to see Caroline pointing his dad's gun at Bobbi.

"Get away from my husband," Caroline yelled.

"New Orleans PD. Everyone, drop the weapons." Emilia stood in the doorway with her own firearm drawn.

Senator Phelps grabbed Bobbi, held her in front of him as a shield, and held his gun at her head. "No way am I dropping it."

"I *will* shoot you if you don't," Emilia said. She didn't waver. Linc was terrified that she would hit Bobbi, even if she didn't intend to.

"It's two against one," Caroline said. "I'm going to

shoot Linc while you're focusing on that girl. What can you do? You can only cover one of us at a time." She turned the gun toward Linc.

Thankful that the woman was stupid enough to tell Emilia what she planned to do, Linc prepared to move aside when Caroline swung the gun in his direction.

Somehow in the next moment, as if in slow motion, Emilia stepped farther into the room, Howard came in behind her, and a couple of shots were fired. Linc darted to one side but his left arm seared in pain. He glanced down to see blood pouring down to his wrist. He looked toward where Bobbi and the senator were to find that the senator was on the floor with a hole in the middle of his forehead. Bobbi was crawling toward Linc with a horrified look on her face.

Caroline yelled, "You killed my husband," right as another shot went off knocking her weapon from her hand. She grabbed her wrist and cried out.

Howard covered the space between them in two seconds flat, picked up the gun Caroline had retrieved from the desk, and pulled out his handcuffs. "You're under arrest, Mrs. Phelps."

Emilia was on her radio calling for ambulances. The room was suddenly filled with cops as the backup team had apparently arrived.

Linc smiled at Bobbi then glanced over at Emilia. "I think I'm going to pass out. How bad am I hit?" It was the last thing he said before everything went black.

Chapter 21

The interrogation went better than Emilia thought it would. Caroline Phelps initially didn't know whether to be the aggrieved widow of the senator and threaten to sue the city of New Orleans over his wrongful death or to blame it all on him. Since he was dead and wouldn't be disputing her tale, she seemed to finally settle on being thought the victim of his nefarious schemes. She settled into telling her story as if her husband was the architect of the plan from the inception until the end. Emilia thought the woman could have won many awards for acting if she'd taken a different career path than murderer. Yes, Caroline could wail and cry crocodile tears with the best of them

Emilia asked Caroline Phelps a few questions, trying her best not to think about Linc and his injury. After a couple of rounds with the senator's wife, Emilia decided to leave her alone in the interrogation room for an hour or two to let her stew a bit before continuing the questioning. Emilia was also waiting for Howard to come back to the station.

When he returned, it was going to be almost too easy to lead the woman down the merry path of letting her make up a bunch of baloney, then to slap her with the truth that they uncovered when he went out with some other detectives and did a sweep of all the hookers in the quarter and questioned them. He scored big when he found one particular prostitute who was a font of knowledge.

Howard showed the woman a picture of Caroline Eisenger Phelps. She immediately recognized her and shared all the information she had. When Howard tossed his notes on Emilia's desk, he said, "Have fun with this one."

"Really? Did you get me some good stuff?" Emilia flipped through his pad. Good thing she could read his writing. She skimmed over the words, her smile growing bigger by the moment. When she'd read them all, she looked up at Howard. "Too bad we didn't find *Miss Hooker Who Knows It All* earlier."

"Yeah, I know. If we'd found her after the first prostitute was killed, Van Nuys might still be around."

"Sadly, I think you're right. Let me take this in and then we'll take her down." Emilia waved Howard's notebook in the air. "Be ready to get the state attorney general on the phone." She stood.

"Why are we doing that? You don't need him in order to charge her."

"I'm thinking about trying to get Myles Eisenger home in time for the Saints game on Saturday."

"Don't get ahead of yourself and get cocky. One step at a time, missy."

"Spoilsport." Emilia stuck her tongue out at Howard and strode toward the interrogation room. Once inside, she pulled out one of the metal chairs, flipped it around, and sat astride it. "Hello, Mrs. Phelps."

"What's that smirk on your face? You have nothing on me. I told you. It was all the senator's idea. I have no part in any of this."

"I think you do."

Caroline crossed her arms. "Your thoughts are not my concern."

"Let me see," Emilia flipped pages in Howard's notebook. "It appears that around the time of Myles's arrest, a woman meeting your description was seen at the edge of the French Quarter on the corner of Esplanade and Burgundy. She was talking to Simon Bolger and she was also seen handing the man a wad of cash."

"That's ridiculous. I don't even know anyone named Simon and, besides, what kind of description would it be? A blonde woman with an expensive haircut, a nice manicure, and a thousand dollar suit? There's a really good chance that many nicely dressed women would be on Esplanade Avenue at any particular time."

"But this is the woman the witness described." Emilia slapped down a picture of Caroline on the table. Emilia was thrilled at the twack sound it made as it hit the top of the table.

Caroline leaned over and studied the photo. "Where'd you get that picture?"

"You're all over the papers, lady. Remember that senator you were trying to blame all this on? When you marry a politician, your picture tends to make the papers. Can you imagine that?"

"You're such a rude young woman. I bet your captain would look down on you talking to me in this manner."

"I think you need to adjust your expectations about the way people will be speaking to you now. Inmates don't get quite the deference that senator's wives do." Emilia smiled and held her hand up. "But wait, I have more."

Caroline exhaled a huge breath. "More what?"

"More nails for your coffin."

"Please. You have nothing. Like I said, I don't know a Simon."

"I also have a witness who can place you at the scene of the crime where that prostitute was killed about two weeks ago."

"What exactly do you think I would be doing with a hooker?" Caroline asked, with an edge of annoyance in her voice.

"Murdering her."

"*What?* You've clearly lost your mind."

"I think not. The girl you killed was with the witness who saw you with Bolger. The two of them saw the transaction with him and, a year or so after Myles was convicted with the help of Bolger's testimony, Bolger ran into these witnesses in the Quarter. And when they asked him about you—because they recognized you as the senator's wife—he got cold feet and called you. You then took care of the one witness and tried to take out the second but you beat on the wrong woman. That woman has been in a coma but guess what? She woke up today. I have someone on the way to the hospital to show her this same picture."

A loud noise in the lobby caught both of their attentions. Emilia stood. "Hang on. Let me see what's going on. I'll be back. Think about what I've said. You may want to adjust your story."

Emilia opened the door. Across the room, a man in a shiny brown suit and an old fashioned bowler hat was cuffed behind the back and cursing at the detective hauling him in. "What's going on?" Emilia called out.

"We got Simon Bolger for you, Hammond. Where do you want him?"

"Park him in interrogation two. I'll deal with him in a little while. May as well offer him some coffee while he waits. I may be a while."

Emilia turned back to Caroline. She knew her grin

was ear to ear. She was that gleeful. "You hear that? Simon Bolger is in the house."

"I want a lawyer." Caroline sat back in the chair with a defiant look on her face. Only her eyes gave her away. She was scared and scared bad.

Emilia wished she could feel sorry for the woman but Caroline had killed too many people in the name of greed for Emilia to muster any pity for her at all.

She stalked over to the table, leaned on it with the knuckles of both hands, and glared into the lady's eyes. "You got it, honey. Let me just call a public defender for you."

"Very funny. Call the senior partner at Cummings and Reichman. They will be my lawyers."

"I wouldn't be so sure of that, Mrs. Phelps."

Caroline leaned forward and actually bared her teeth at Emilia. "Why would you say that?"

"You're not going to have the money to pay them their high fees."

"And why not? I'm a wealthy widow. Twice widowed, in fact. Once because of you."

"Ah, but you see, Linc is almost convinced to open the family crypt to see if Oliver Eisenger was helped to his death and, if so, there will be no money there for you since murderers don't get to benefit from their bad behavior. As for the senator, his money will be frozen until the courts can figure out his part in this. The funds will be put on hold for their use in victim's reparations."

"You can't do that." Caroline practically shrieked the words.

"Watch me, baby, watch me." Emilia turned and strolled out the interrogation room door. Before she shut it, she called out, "Someone call for a public defender for this woman."

She closed the door to the sound of Caroline's sobs. She was pretty sure that the woman was crying for her own position not for the loss of lives she'd caused.

Emilia walked over to the room next door where Bolger awaited his own session with her.

ৎ৲৩৴৩

Linc sat on the curtained-off bed in the emergency room cubicle. Light-headed and a bit loopy from the pain medications that the doctor gave him before sewing up the gash from where the bullet grazed his upper arm, he smiled at Bobbi. "Too bad you can't drive yet. You could take me home."

"I can drive. Hand me the keys and we'll check you out of here." She grinned and held her hand out for them.

"Very funny. I meant you can't as you're only fourteen not that you don't know how."

"Who cares? We've been through a heck of a day and we still have to deal with my status here in Louisiana tomorrow. Shouldn't we get you home to rest?"

"We'll have to wait until these meds wear off. You

may as well grab my wallet from my slacks over there and get a few dollars to buy a magazine at the gift shop. Something to pass the time, you know." Linc rubbed his arm as it lay in the sling. "I still don't know why I need this."

"The doctor said that you had to hold that arm still for a few days and that would help."

"Yeah, I know what he said but I still think it's needless."

"Mr. Eisenger?" A hand drew back the curtain. Greta Greensboro poked her head inside. "I heard the news. Can I help?"

"What did you hear?" Linc wasn't sure he wanted to speak to Greta. He was still suspicious of her—and why she seemed to be spying on him. Was she in on the murders?

Greta stepped all the way in to the cubicle. "That your mother's husband was killed and that she's a suspect in the murders of Van Nuys and that young girl."

"And you heard this *where*?"

"It's all over the news. It's on the television. Every channel it seems. A big scandal. Huge."

"Do you have any other information?"

Greta blushed. "In what way?"

"In any way. Do you know something that could help the police?"

"I'm not sure, to be honest."

"Why don't you tell me what you think you know so

I can pass it on to the detectives? I can see if they think your information would help in the investigation. I confess, I've been thinking that you know more about all this than you've said."

Greta placed a hand on the mattress where Linc sat. "Why?"

"It seems to me that you've been keeping tabs on me for the last several months and it has me concerned."

"Your mother asked me to keep an eye on you. She said that since Myles was convicted that you seemed erratic as well as suicidal. She told me that you'd been hiring hookers—"

Bobbi gasped. "Linc would never to that. He wants to help those of us on the streets."

"Let her go on, Bobbi. I have a feeling this is important." Linc waggled his fingers to urge Greta to go on. "What else?"

"She said you had been violent at her house toward the senator and that she was worried about you. If Myles's appeals failed, she was concerned that you would kill yourself or maybe go off the deep end and hurt someone else. She asked me to let her know if you showed any sign of instability."

"And you *believed* her?" Bobbi demanded. "How long have you worked for Linc that you could, for one second, believe any of that junk? He's a good man and would never hurt anyone *or* himself. I've only known him a couple of days and I know this about him to the depths of my soul. What kind of assistant are you to think this crazy story that woman told you could be true?" She was practically lathering at the mouth.

"It's all right, Bobbi. I appreciate you for coming to my defense but let's let Greta tell us all she knows about Caroline Phelps." He nodded at his assistant. "Go on."

"She came in and met with Van Nuys a few times."

Linc nodded. "Do you know what about?"

Greta turned red again. "I'm sorry but I do."

"It's all right. Tell me what she was doing there. You won't get in trouble." Linc's heart leaped in hope. Maybe Greta had something to offer that would help convict Caroline of his former partner's murder.

"She had a lot of questions about your family trust. She brought it in one day for Clifford to review. They met a couple of times about it. She was focused on—" Greta smacked herself in the forehead. "Gee, I'm an idiot. What a fool I've been."

"We've already established that, lady."

"Bobbi." Linc looked a threat at the girl. "Stop." He nodded at Greta.

"She was focused on how the trust would end. She wanted to know how and when the principal would be disbursed." Linc could tell when Greta realized what was going on as she went ashen and her hands went to her cheeks. "Oh my God, Mr. Eisenger, she was going to *kill* you. She wanted the money. Oh Lord, and you think I was helping her, don't you?" Tears ran down Greta's face. "You know I'd never go along with that. *Don't* you?"

"I admit I had my doubts, Greta, especially when I was in the conference room with Detective Hammond."

"I'm so sorry. Please don't fire me."

"I'm not going to fire you but I'm going to call Detective Mills as I think he's going to want to talk to you." Linc pointed to his slacks. "Grab my phone out of my front pocket, Bobbi."

"Why Detective Mills and not Hammond? Does she hate me?" Greta asked while Bobbi tried to get to Linc's phone.

"I don't think she hates you but, even if she did, she wouldn't let that stand in the way of her professionalism."

Bobbi let out a guffaw at that and, with a flourish, handed Linc his phone.

"Let me make this call, get checked out of here, and after you drive me and Bobbi home, Greta, maybe you can go over and see the detective."

"I will and I'll be sure to tell him everything I know. I still can't believe that your mother is such a wicked, wicked woman."

"That woman is *not* my mother." Linc growled the words out as he poked in Howard Mills' number on his phone.

Chapter 22

By Friday afternoon, Emilia was really ready for the weekend. The last few days had been spent in a flurry of tying up loose ends on the case against Caroline, visiting Linc as he recovered at home and worked on his project of keeping Bobbi in New Orleans, as well as getting a hearing set to have Myles released from prison. She'd even been on the morning talk shows in the area to tell how the case had broken open. It seemed the senator was in on the crimes as deep as his wife was. The media was in a frenzy about it and Emilia was exhausted with the whole thing.

Linc had consented to the opening of the family crypt and having his father's body exhumed. Upon the opening, they'd found his mother, Samantha, as well. Linc asked the medical examiner to take them both to the morgue and see if he could determine what had really happened to his biological mother. He had a feeling that the nanny, Caroline, had helped her to her demise. It wouldn't surprise him to find that the woman he'd called mother for his entire life had planned and executed the murder of the woman who was his real mother. If he could make her go down for that as well, then he was going to arrange it.

Emilia picked Linc and Bobbi up from his house after lunch on Friday to attend the hearing where the attorney general would be asking the court to dismiss all charges against Myles. It was a formality but Linc wanted them all to be there for the moment when his brother became a free man. Linc still wasn't allowed to drive but the doctor said he'd be able to stop using the sling the next day. He couldn't wait and would already have taken it off but Bobbi was quite the little taskmaster and forced him to leave it on.

Bobbi's own court hearing had gone well. The man who purported to be her father didn't appear. Linc presumed it was because Rhodes warned him not to. It was all right, though, since the local judge spoke to a judge in Minnesota and they agreed to allow Bobbi to stay in Louisiana under the protection of family services with placement in Linc's custody. As he predicted, there was no problem with him being a single man, especially after Bobbi testified that he'd rescued her from a life on the streets.

Linc had spent a portion of the week talking to the trustees at the bank about changing the use of the old

Carmelite nunnery the trust owned to a facility to assist the street kids. A portion of it was presently being used as a small café but Linc assured the trustees that he and Myles could work around that.

Emilia's car pulled in front of the courthouse. There was a massive knot of reporters gathered for the press conference afterward. "I thought I could let you two off here and park in the back but you don't want to get out in this mess. I'll drive around."

"No, Emilia. I want to get out here and stroll past these people. These are the same folks who were ready to have Myles executed for a crime he didn't commit. I want to hold my head high and walk silently past them with them asking if I have anything to say."

"You're crazy, you know that right?" Bobbi asked.

"It's part of the Eisenger charm. Both of you need to get used to it. You'll be subjected to a double dose once you meet Myles." Linc winked at Emilia. "We'll see you inside. Come on, Bobbi."

Linc and Bobbi got out of the car and stepped on the sidewalk. Emilia watched their progress through the crowd for a moment and then went to park.

She entered the courthouse through the back doors reserved for law enforcement and made her way to the courtroom, arriving in time to be told by the bailiff that it was standing room only. He didn't want to let her in but finally agreed when she told him she had a reserved seat.

Emilia walked down the aisle between the pew-like

benches and found Linc and Bobbi in the pew right behind the defense counsel table in the front row. Sure
enough, they'd saved her a seat. She made it to their row
and took her spot at the very moment the judge walked
into the court room. After the bailiff called court to order
and everyone rose, the judge took the bench and instruct-
ed everyone to be seated.

"The case of The State of Louisiana versus Myles
Robert Eisenger is the only case on the docket today.
Does the prosecution have a motion to make?" The judge
looked at the lawyer from the attorney general's office.

"Yes, sir." The lawyer for the state stood. "The State
of Louisiana moves to dismiss all charges against the de-
fendant, Myles Eisenger as it has been shown beyond a
reasonable doubt that he could not have committed the
crime he's been accused and convicted of committing.
The state believes it has the true culprit in custody who
will be charged with the homicide as soon as these charges are dismissed."

The judge turned to Myles' lawyer. "Does the defense have anything to add?"

Myles' lawyer stood. "Other than to ask the court to
make his release immediate so that he can accompany his
family home, no, sir."

"Case dismissed with prejudice." The judge slammed
his gavel on the table then stared down at Myles. "Mr.
Eisenger, on behalf of the State of Louisiana, let me be
the first to apologize to you for your unlawful incarcera-

tion and to wish you all the best for your future. You're free to return home right now."

The judge stood and stepped out of the courtroom as the place erupted in cheers from the gallery. Myles turned around and reached for his brother. Linc hugged him over the bar separating the well of the court from the gallery. Emilia watched with tears in her eyes. These two men were all that were left of the Eisenger family and she was thrilled to have been a part of getting them back together where they belonged and not on either side of prison bars.

She also had a secret and she hoped that the two of them would be as excited as she was about it when she revealed it to them.

After a few moments, without letting go of his brother completely, Linc half-turned to glance at Emilia and Bobbi. "Come over and meet Myles."

The smile on Linc's face glowed and took Emilia's breath away. She'd never seen him appear so young and carefree. The burden of his brother's incarceration had clearly sat heavy on his soul. He seemed to have lost ten years of age in the last five minutes. Even the lines around his mouth looked smoother.

Emilia pushed Bobbi ahead of her. "It seems right that Myles gets to say hello first to his new foster niece."

Myles enveloped the girl in a hug. He looked over her head at Emilia. "I hear I owe you a debt of gratitude, Detective Hammond."

"Call me Emilia."

She held her hand out to be shaken but Myles ignored it. He let go of Bobbi and pulled Emilia into a tight hug.

When he turned her loose, Myles smiled. "I don't know about you three but I'm ready to get out of here and start to live life again."

"Sounds like a plan to me, little brother. I have you staying with me for now. Your house was rented out by the trust at the insistence of that woman Caroline almost as soon as you were incarcerated. Since those folks have about six months left on their lease, I moved you into my place. Your furniture and everything like that is still in the storage facility but your clothes and all that are at my house." Linc led Myles over to the swinging gate that led to the gallery. "Hurry up. Time's a wasting."

"I'll stay with you tonight, bro, but I'd rather move into the First Street house since it's vacant now that Caroline's in jail. Do you think that would be all right?"

"Since you're the last beneficiaries of the trust, Linc, shouldn't the trustees allow Myles to live wherever he wants?" Emilia asked.

They all, including Myles's attorney, walked down the aisle past the seats in the courtroom. Several people high-fived or knuckle-bumped Myles as they went.

A woman ran up and hugged Linc. "I'm so happy you got your brother freed. My friends and I saw it in the papers and wanted to come wish him well."

Stepping back from the hug, Linc looked astounded.

He turned to his brother. "Hang on a second. This is Patsy. I met her at the rodeo." He grinned at the woman. "Well, hello there. Sorry I can't show you the town today but I have a brother to take home."

"I know that, silly man. We merely wanted to share in your joy and make sure to invite you back to the rodeo to sit with us again in the spring." Patsy patted his arm and tilted her head toward her friends. They all nodded and waved.

"I appreciate it but I'm not sure I'll ever go back up there. Too many bad memories, you know, but it does mean a lot to me that you ladies made the trip and fought the crowds to wish my family well." He kissed her on the cheek. "I have to be going now."

"I know. Be careful, and *do* let us know if you change your mind." Patsy strolled off with her pals.

The crowd had pushed closer as Linc spoke to Patsy. He took hold of Emilia's hand with his free one and used his elbow in the sling to clear space in the mass of well-wishers for the five of them to walk.

He picked up their conversation about the trust and a place to live for Myles. "I think the trustees will let him reside in whatever property he desires. Not to change the subject, but one of the things I need to talk about with you, Emilia, is the fact that I am one of the last two Eisengers."

"And why is that a concern of mine?" Emilia asked. "Other than to try to prevent someone else from trying to get rid of you boys in order to get their mitts on your property and money."

They stepped through the double doors from the courtroom and into the corridor. Linc stopped in the middle of the hallway ignoring the people all around yelling questions at Myles and his defense lawyer. Linc stared down at Emilia. "This may not be the time and place to say this, but I'm counting on you to help me not be the last of the Eisengers."

He grinned, then—as she gaped at him, trying to determine what the heck he meant—Linc grabbed his brother's attorney's arm. "Come on, man, let's get to that blasted press conference so I can take my brother home and fatten him up."

The three men and the young girl walked in front of her toward the exit. Emilia stood in shock as she watched them go.

ℰℐℰℐ

The next afternoon Emilia's surprise guests arrived. She and Alyce-Faye met them at the Algiers ferry parking lot and rode across the river on the ferry. Emilia didn't ride the free ride very often but she wanted to today. She wanted to enjoy the time on the river to get to know her guests as well as to ask some questions about the past.

Her parents planned a big bash to celebrate Myles's

freedom and the trip on the ferry to the party was the first chance Emilia had to have a nice chat with her company. Emilia's folks arranged to have a shrimp and crawfish boil in their back yard and invited a big crowd. That was the way it was done in their town. Get the biggest pots you could find and, once the water came to a boil, add some Zatarains seasonings bags, jumbo shrimp, crawfish, new potatoes, and corn on the cob.

The only other requirements were a couple of long tables fetched from the church fellowship hall and a few rolls of butcher paper to cover the tables so that the only clean-up was to wad up that paper and toss it in the garbage can.

Upon arrival at the dock on the Algiers side, Emilia's grandfather, Emil, and father, Douglas, met them. Emil scooped Emilia up in a bear hug. "Here's my granddaughter the detective." He spun her around.

"Put me down, you big oaf." Emilia pummeled him on the chest. "I have company I want you to meet."

Emil put her down and turned to her guests. "Of course, I know my favorite psychic here, Alyce-Faye but I haven't had the pleasure of meeting you other folks."

"Granddad, this is Linc and Myles Eisenger's grandparents, Anna and Bernard Brooks, as well as two cousins, Jake and Frank."

"Let's get you loaded in the cars and over to the house. I know everyone will be thrilled to meet you all." Emil led the four of them to his SUV.

Emilia's dad glanced over at her and Alyce-Faye and pointed to his sedan. "Do the Eisenger's know you invited their relatives?"

"No. They have no idea."

"Is that a good plan? What if there's some bad blood or something? You don't know what the deal is."

"What makes you think there might be a problem?"

Emilia was truly confused. She'd talked to her dad about finding Linc's relatives and he acted as if he wanted her to do that. They walked toward the car.

"I have no idea if there will be. When you said you were going to see if you could find them and see why they never came around when the Eisenger boys were growing up, I never dreamed you'd take it on yourself to invite them today. I figured you'd have your chat, then tell Linc what you learned and leave it to him to make contact."

Emilia stopped in her tracks. "Crap. You're right. I'm stupid. Freak. What am I going to do now?"

"It's going to be fine, Emilia. Don't fret," Alyce-Faye said.

"Are you saying that as a platitude or as a psychic?" Emilia asked.

"A little bit of both."

Emilia stalked over to the passenger side of her father's car and opened the door. "That doesn't make me any happier."

"However it plays out, it's in motion now," Douglas said as he got in on the driver's side.

The drive to her parents' place seemed shorter than ever as Emilia fretted over her decision to invite the Brookses to the party.

When they all arrived and made their way to the back yard, Emilia was stunned to see a huge number of people standing around under the overhead crisscrossed wires where someone had hung numerous light bulbs. The yard was illuminated in a romantic way that made Emilia take a deep breath. As she glanced around at the guests, she was more than shocked to see her precinct captain, her co-workers, and even the mayor.

She turned to her grandfather who was right beside her. "What's this all about? I thought this was a family party to celebrate Myles being freed." She nodded at the two Eisenger men who stood to one side of the mayor. Both of them wore huge grins.

"Come on out in the yard. You can introduce your guests to their family after the mayor has a word with you." Emil led her out to the center of the area near the boiling pots.

The mayor walked over and shook Emilia's hand. Behind him stood Emilia's captain. The crowd got quiet with all eyes on the four of them.

The mayor cleared his throat and turned to the side so that he and Emilia were facing the group. "Detective Hammond, this is a commendation—" He took a plaque from the captain's hands. "—for, as your first assignment since earning your gold shield, your meritorious service in solving four murders and one assault and battery. There's also a strong possibility that a fifth case that wasn't even suspected to be a murder may be solved as well. That's going to be a hard record to break, young lady." He handed her the plaque.

The crowd clapped and then chanted, "Speech, speech."

Embarrassed, Emilia ducked her head. Her grandfather whispered, "Own it, baby. You earned it. Give them what they want."

She smiled at him for his encouragement, took the plaque, and raised it above her head. She really was stunned at the award but it made her realize she was a good detective. She also realized the mayor miscounted the number of cases she and Mills had solved. Mills's name popping in her head reminded her of him and the lack of a commendation for him.

Forgetting protocol, she turned to the mayor. "What about Detective Mills? Where's his? He did as much work as I did."

Howard stepped up. "I got one, too, Em, but I wanted you to have your moment in the sun so to speak. You deserve the recognition as it is an admirable thing that you did on your first case."

"But we solved three murders, not four." She counted them on her fingers, "One was the clerk Myles was accused of killing, the next was the young prostitute, and then Van Nuys."

"You also solved Mr. Oliver Eisenger's murder. He was definitely poisoned before he drowned," the mayor said.

"I thought you meant his death when you said we'd solved one that wasn't known to be a murder," Emilia shook her head.

"We won't know for a few weeks when some more intensive toxicology reports come back but Samantha Brooks may well have been dead before she was hung which would mean it wasn't a suicide. Since she's been in the crypt so long, there needed to be different tests run but the medical examiner is pretty certain that something will be found." The captain shook her hand. "Well done, Detective."

Emilia's gaze flew toward Samantha's parents. She needed to tell them this news. "Will you all excuse me, please?"

She made a beeline toward Samantha's family who were standing with Alyce-Faye by the table that held tall urns of sweet tea, regular tea, and coffee, both caffeinated and decaf.

Before she got to them, Linc and Myles waylaid her. Linc leaned down and kissed her on the cheek. "Way to go. A commendation on your first case. Sounds like the makings of a great career."

"Linc, I have something I need to do and some people you and Myles need to meet. I hope you won't be mad at me but I had to do it, and now I'm glad I did, even if you hate me forever."

"I have no idea what you're talking about but I know one thing. I could never hate you." Linc took hold of her elbow. "Now, where are these people you want me to meet?"

She took a deep breath and led him and Myles over to his grandparents and cousins. As soon as they were in front of them, Anna Brooks began to cry as she looked first from one man to the other. She held her hand up as if to touch Myles's face but pulled back at the last second. She turned her head toward Emilia. Her eyes practically begged Emilia to make this all work out the way she wanted it to.

Behind her, Emilia heard her father call out, "Come on, everyone. It's time to turn out the food. We need some strong guys to help carry the pots."

Glad of the diversion, Emilia said, "Let's all move aside. Some of those folks are going to want tea in a minute."

When she had them all in an isolated spot, she nodded at the Brookses. "Linc and Myles, these people are your mother's parents and your two cousins. Anna and Bernard Brooks, Jake and Frank Brooks."

"*What?*" Both Eisenger men said at the same time.

"I'm sorry I sprang it on you here but I wasn't thinking how it would go over when I invited them." She turned to the Brookses. "The captain also just told me that the medical examiner thinks your daughter may not have committed suicide, after all."

Anna grabbed her chest and Emilia noticed her knees almost give way. Linc reached out, took his grandmother by the waist, and held her up. "That's a good thing. That means she didn't want to leave us."

"I never thought my darling girl would've done such a thing, but each time I came to try to find out something, that woman Caroline would turn me away." Mrs. Brooks' voice quavered. "When it first happened, your father was so shattered that he could barely communicate. I think that's how he ended up married to that woman. He started to rely on her for everything and it was easier to marry her than to make any decisions."

"Why didn't you come see us? Why didn't we know about you?" Myles asked.

"We tried. We wanted to be part of your lives but every time we'd call, Caroline would say you weren't home. If we drove over, she wouldn't let us in. Then one day, we got an injunction served on us that we weren't allowed to try to contact you again," Bernard said.

"What about when we became adults?" Linc asked.

"We figured as long as that woman was around that she'd poisoned you against us. Once you became adults and were no longer under her influence, we expected you to contact us. We waited and waited but you never did. We assumed you didn't want to meet us because you never called or wrote. We assumed Caroline had succeeded in making you think we didn't love you. We had no idea that you didn't even know you had a mother who adored you both to pieces. This young lady let us know that when she called. We'd like to have you as a part of the family more than anything on earth, but we will understand if you hate us for not trying harder when you were children." Bernard did the talking, as his wife seemed as if she were going to collapse. He held on to her under her forearm.

Linc appeared to realize his grandmother needed assistance at the same time Emilia did. He darted off and came back with a chair for her. When she was seated, he knelt down in front of her. "Do you need some water, Grandmother?"

She burst into tears as soon as he called her Grandmother.

He patted her knee and glanced over at his newly met cousins. "Can one of you fetch some water?"

Jake ran off to do Linc's bidding. Emilia's father came over. "Come eat. These scoundrels may get it all if you don't hurry."

"I don't know if I can eat. There's been too much excitement," Anna said.

"You can and will." Douglas stepped around Linc and held his hand out to Anna. "Let's get a place at the table for you all. There will be plenty of time to catch up with your grandsons. A lifetime indeed."

"You know, that shrimp does smell divine." Anna smiled and let Douglas lead her to the table. The others followed until Emilia was left standing alone with Linc.

He smiled. "You sure are full of surprises, Detective."

"So you don't hate me?"

"Never." Linc took her hand. "I could never hate the amazing, the lovely, the incredibly gifted Detective Emilia Hammond."

"Wow, that's a lot of adjectives."

"It takes a lot of them to describe you, my dear, dear Emilia."

The three-piece jazz band made up of Emilia's two brothers and her grandfather, who played two nights a week at Preservation Hall, struck up a tune. They stood on the back porch of the house and played a snappy zydeco tune.

"Would you dance with me?" Linc asked.

"Only if you promise to take me out to eat when we're done."

"There's a ton of food here. Why do I need to take you out?"

"If I'm going to dance with you, all that food will be gone before we're done. I know these people. They're all about the eating. So you have a choice to make. Pay for food later and I'll dance with you or let me eat now and miss the dancing."

"Since I can't wait to hold you in my arms, I guess

I'm going to have to come up with some dollars to feed you."

Emilia winked at him as he pulled her into his embrace. "I hear you have a trust fund. You can afford it."

The dance floor, which was actually a cleared spot in the grass, quickly became crowded with other couples. Linc spun Emilia around in time with the music and in a short while, she found herself still in his arms and behind her father's workshop.

"What are you doing? Why are we back here?"

"I keep finding myself in the situation where I can't kiss you uninterrupted and I'm tired of it. I'm going to put my lips on yours and I am not going to take them off until you're swooning in my arms. Bet on it."

"You know, I would've slept with you that night at your house but you got all puritanical on me with Bobbi being in the house and now you have her there full time. When did you ever expect us to have a chance to be alone?"

"Right now. Behind the woodshed."

She couldn't help herself. She laughed out loud. "With about eighty people on the other side."

"I can see I'm going to have to find a way to keep you quiet if we don't want those eighty people finding us."

With those words, he captured her lips with his exactly as he'd promised. She opened her mouth to allow his tongue access and he kissed her until her knees gave way and she *did* swoon. Before she was quite done with the swooning thing, Myles came around the corner. He tapped Linc on the shoulder and the kiss ended.

"I'm going to take the family back to get their car and ask them to stay over tonight at your place. You have plenty of space, after all. I'll take Bobbi with me. You and your lady-love here can either get a room at the local inn or go back to her place. I'll watch your ward so you can have some alone time with the detective." Myles grinned.

"What's that smile all about?" Emilia asked.

"Only that everyone out there knows you two are back here canoodling."

Linc laughed. "Oh God, Emilia. I've compromised your integrity. I guess I'll have to marry you."

"Yeah, right." She winked. "Although you *did* say something at the courthouse yesterday that made me wonder what you meant."

"My comment about needing help to not be the last of the Eisengers?"

"Exactly." Emilia really did want to know what he meant.

"Not that I'm asking for children in the next year or so but I sure would like to have a few before I'm forty. Is nine years long enough?"

"You *can't* be serious. You've known me a week. Quit messing around and let's get out of here so my family and half the precinct can stop gossiping about me."

"I'm not kidding, Emilia. I know what I want and I want *you*."

"Let's talk about that later. There's plenty of time for that."

"A lifetime, my dear." With that, Linc scooped her into his arms and, followed by Myles, carried her from behind the workshop and through the crowd. He nodded to various people in the yard as he took her out through the gate.

She laughed at the stunned expressions on everyone's faces and knew that she was going to spend a lifetime being amused by this man. This man she once thought was arrogant and unkind and who she now knew to have a heart and soul of purity and grace and, yes, a man she'd grown to love in a mere week.

The End

About the Author

Sherry Fowler Chancellor is a practicing attorney who lives on the beautiful Gulf Coast of Florida. When she's not working on behalf of her clients, she's busy penning a new story or hanging out with her friends and family in their own little slice of paradise.